Bug Out! Part 2

Civilization in Peril

Robert Boren

South Bay Press

Author/Publishing South Bay Press

Book Layout ©2017 BookDesignTemplates.com
Cover Design: SelfPubBookCovers.com/RLSather
Bug Out! Part 2– Civilization in Peril/ Robert Boren. – 3rd ed.
ISBN 9781973387763

For Elliot

Take time to deliberate; but when the time for action arrives, stop thinking and go in.

—Andrew Jackson

Contents

Previously – in Part 1: 1

The Next Level...3

No Safe Harbor 17

Special Bulletin 31

TV Night 45

Watch the Perimeter...59

Back in the Woods 73

Up in the Blinds 87

Security 101

Happy Hour..115

To Trust or Not To Trust...129

Was it Murder?...141

Previously – in Part 1:

Frank and Jane escaped from California just before the border was shut down. On the road they saw military convoys with tanks rolling south. They made it to Quartzsite, Arizona, but things were too crazy there, and they had to leave after one night. They stopped outside Williams, Arizona, but had to get back onto the road again after an altercation where Frank shot a corrupt Police Officer named Simmons. Radical Militia leaders tried to force our heroes and their fellow travelers to a location where they would be relieved of their guns and supplies. Led by Frank, they fought their way out and made it to a friendly place near the Grand Canyon. They thought it was finally time to relax. They were wrong. An Army officer and a Police officer tracked them down and confronted them.

The Next Level

Frank and Jane got out of the pool and picked up their towels. Jane felt naked in her bathing suit as the Police Officer and the Army Officer watched her dry off. Frank sensed that, and placed himself in front of her, blocking their view.

"You guys can use the clubhouse to talk," Charlie said. He walked towards the doors, with the two officers following him.

When Frank and Jane got through the door, the officers were sitting on one side of the first row of benches, and motioned for them to sit down on the opposite side. Charlie was puttering around in the other side of the large room, trying to remain within earshot.

"Sorry to bother you two," the police officer said. "I'm officer Bannon. This is Lieutenant Humphrey from the US Army."

"Good to meet you both," Frank said. "I guess you already know who we are."

"Don't be worried. You two aren't in any trouble. We know there were some issues with the Williams police department. Why were you two in Williams?"

Frank collected his thoughts.

"We decided to leave Southern California for a while, to escape the looting and gang violence," he said.

"It was getting too close to our house, and there was an incident the night before we left," Jane added.

"An incident?" asked Officer Bannon.

"Yes," Jane said. "The looters came down our street. A few of them came up our driveway, and were getting ready to break in when Frank got their attention with a shot gun."

"Did you shoot someone there?" asked Officer Bannon.

"No, I just cocked the gun and told them they had better leave," Frank said. "They were just kids. They ran away."

"So I take it you two took I-10 and came up through southern Arizona?" asked Lieutenant Humphrey.

"Yes," Jane said. "We were hoping to stay in Quartzsite for a while, but we heard bad things about the border nearby, and about Yuma."

"Was Williams a destination, or just a stopover point for you?" asked Officer Bannon.

"Just a stopover. We are planning to continue to the north," Frank said. "This place is a stopover too, although we like it here."

"Well, we are hoping to make this area safe in the near future, but I don't blame you two for wanting to go a little further north," Lieutenant Humphrey said.

"How did you two come to meet Dave Jacobsen?" asked Officer Bannon.

"Didn't know his last name until now," Frank said. "He came running into our camp after his police chief shot himself in an RV that was near us."

"So you didn't know him before that?" asked Lieutenant Humphrey.

"No," Jane said.

"Did he have anybody with him when you met him?" asked Lieutenant Humphrey.

"Yes," Frank said. "A young kid named Ken, and a guy in his mid-30s named Lewis."

"Good, that checks out," Officer Bannon said. "We found Dave Jacobsen's body near Ken's body, and a jeep that rolled over several times."

"They're both dead?" asked Jane.

"Yes. What can you tell us about that?"

"They were trying to get us to stop on the highway," Frank said. "Ken had a rifle on us. We wouldn't stop, and either would any of the other coaches in the group that was following us."

"So how did they end up running off the road?" asked Officer Bannon.

"They were alongside us, in the southbound lane. A semi-truck came down the road towards them. They had only two choices – force us over or drive off the shoulder on the southbound side to avoid a head on collision with the semi. I wasn't letting him move me over. He drove onto the shoulder going too fast, and cartwheeled."

"Why didn't you want to stop for him?" asked Lieutenant Humphrey.

"We had reason to believe they were herding us towards a militia group, in order to steal our supplies and weapons," Jane said.

"That's exactly what they were planning on doing," Lieutenant Humphrey said.

"How do you know that?" asked Frank.

"We captured the third person, and it came out in the interrogation," he replied.

"Lewis?" asked Jane.

"Yes."

"What's going to happen to him?" asked Frank.

"He'll probably be shot for treason," Lieutenant Humphrey said. "You folks are lucky that you got away from these guys."

"Is that all you needed to talk to them about, Lieutenant Humphrey?" asked Officer Bannon.

"Just one other thing," he said. "Do you know anything about an Officer Simmons?"

Frank felt a knot in his throat, and the feeling of panic set in.

"He was shot as we were leaving the campground outside of Williams," Jane said. "He was trying to hold us there, even though he knew the enemy was coming."

"We saw the evidence that he was shot, but not badly," Officer Bannon said. "There was a small amount of blood on the ground, and we found his car off to the side of the road. We think he is still alive. We don't know where he went, though. That is disturbing to us."

"Why?" asked Frank.

"He's working for the enemy, and he's dangerous," he replied. "He's a psychopath. We've been watching him for while. This guy kills people for fun. We need to re-acquire him as quickly as possible."

"Did he join the enemy in the battle that happened there?" asked Frank.

"We don't think so," Lieutenant Humphrey said. "Almost the entire enemy force was burned up in a bombing and napalm attack, and that happened about ½ a mile up the road. They never got all the way to where Officer Simmons was, from what we can tell."

"Do you know who shot him," asked Officer Bannon.

Frank sat silent for a moment, and looked down. Then he looked Officer Bannon in the eye.

"I shot him."

Officer Bannon could see that Frank was waiting for the handcuffs to come out. He smiled.

"Well, it was a nice try, Frank. Wish you would have hit him square in the forehead."

Frank got a surprised look on his face.

"I'm not in trouble?"

"No, Frank, not from us. How good of a look did Simmons get of you?"

"Pretty good," Frank said.

"Then you need to watch yourself. This guy is nuts, and he might come after you folks. You need to keep a low profile, and be watchful."

"He saw our coach," Jane said, with a worried look on her face.

"I figured," Officer Bannon said. "I would go ahead and move north if I were you guys. Officer Simmons's user ids with the police department have been suspended, but he still may have ways of getting info on you. Hopefully he didn't jot down your license plate number. He's nuts, but he's also quite intelligent."

"Crap," Frank said.

The two officers stood up.

"Thanks for being honest with us," Lieutenant Humphrey said.

"And be careful," said Officer Bannon.

They tipped their hats and walked out the door. Charlie walked over.

"Quite a story," Charlie said.

"I'm glad you were here listening to it," Frank said. "I was afraid they were going to kick you out."

"I think we are going to need to go further north," Jane said.

"Yes, I heard that," Charlie said. "I'll refund you for the last two days."

"Thanks," Frank said. "I wish we could stick around."

"We all might have to leave anyway," Charlie said. "I don't like the reports I'm reading about New Mexico. The Texans have the enemy on the run over there, and they might be on their way to this area."

"Yes, I was reading about that before we came over to the pool," Frank said. "Sounds like they are mostly Islamists, too."

"Same thing I read. I'm going to watch for the rest of today and into mid-morning tomorrow. If they are still on their way here and Army reinforcements haven't arrived, I'm outa here."

Frank nodded, and then looked over at Jane.

"Should we go enjoy the pool for a little while longer?" he asked.

"No, I'm too nervous. I think we should go back to the coach and get her ready to leave."

"I'm with you. Let's go. See you later, Charlie."

"Good luck to you folks," he said.

They walked out the door and headed for their RV. As they were walking, Chester saw them and came up.

"I saw you guys go into the clubhouse with the cop and the Army buy. Everything OK?"

"Yes and no," Frank said. "Nobody is in trouble for our little game of chicken with Dave and Ken last night, or the shooting of Officer Simmons.

"Well, that's good. What's the bad news?"

"Officer Simmons has disappeared, and those guys just told me that he's a real psycho. They said he might come after us for shooting him."

"Oh Oh – he's still alive?" Chester asked. "What are you guys going to do?"

"We're heading further north," Jane said.

"When are you folks leaving?"

"Now," Jane said.

"Oh. Well, I guess I can't blame you."

"It's a shame," Frank said. "We would have enjoyed a few days rest here."

Chester looked sad, and was deep in thought.

"Would you folks object to some company?"

"We don't want to organize a large exodus," Jane said, "But we wouldn't have any problem at all with other people tagging along. Why?"

"Charlie told me that there's a possibility we will have some Islamic visitors from the east. I can tell he's worried about it."

"Yeah, he said something about that to us, also," Frank said. "He's going to see how things are by mid-morning tomorrow, and if they are still on the way here without reinforcements showing up, he's going to clear out."

"Well, maybe I ought to wait with him and take off when he does," Chester said. "I owe him that much. Where are you two headed? Maybe we can meet up later."

"We will try to make it up to Capitol Reef, right up by where Route 89 meets up with I-70."

"Well, that's doable before dark if you get going pretty quickly. Lots of nice RV parks up there, too."

"Good," Jane said.

"Oh, forgot to ask. What happened with Dave and Ken and Lewis?"

"Dave and Ken are dead," Frank said. "Lewis got captured. The Army guy told us that they were planning to bring us to their militia and take our supplies and guns. They probably would have killed all of us."

"Wow, I guess we dodged that bullet," Chester said. "Alright, I'll let you guys go do what you need to be doin. Thanks so much for what you did for us yesterday."

"Thank you, Chester," Frank said. Chester nodded, and shook hands with Frank and Jane. Then they continued on to their coach.

"Wonder if we'll see them again?" asked Jane.

"Probably. I don't think this place is going to be safe. I think we are just leaving a little early. The rest of them will be along."

Frank unlocked the door and opened it. Lucy bounded out, tail wagging.

"I'll go walk her, sweetie," Frank said. "Could you start stowing the kitchen stuff, and get the bedroom ready to close up?"

"Of course," she said as she climbed up the steps.

Frank hooked the leash on Lucy and walked her around. Frank noticed that other people were getting ready to leave too. He walked down the end of his row, and saw Jeb getting ready.

"You clearing out?" asked Frank.

"Yup, sure am, and you folks should do the same," Jeb said.

"We are," Frank said. "Right now, in fact."

"Worried about the folks coming from the east too, I suspect."

"Yes. We're going farther north. Planning on making it to Capitol Reef."

"Great minds think alike again," Jeb said, laughing. "I'll be seeing you there. Godspeed." He turned back to what he was doing.

Frank walked back to the coach, and let Lucy in the door. Then he started to break down the chairs and the table. He stowed them in the storage compartment, and then reached into the coach and pushed the button to close the awning. When it was in he walked back into the door.

"Lucy do OK?" asked Jane. She had just changed back into her clothes.

"Yep, perfect dog, as usual," Frank said. "Other people are getting ready to leave now. They're all afraid of the enemy coming from the east."

"You didn't tell them why we were leaving?"

"I didn't mention Officer Simmons, no. I went along with the enemy approaching as a reason, which actually isn't a total lie," Frank said. He changed back into his clothes as they were talking.

"True. You can bring in the bedroom slide now. Mr. Wonderful is up on the front passenger seat."

"Thanks," Frank said. He walked over to the panel and pushed the button. The slide came in slowly. "Done. I'll go out and get the hookups undone."

"Alright. I'm almost ready for the salon slides to come in. I'll go ahead and retract them."

Frank nodded as he walked down the steps. He got the city water and electrical unhooked. The black and grey tanks were still nearly empty, so he just took the hose off and stowed it. He walked around the coach, double checking all of the compartments and looking things over. Then he remembered tire pressure. He went into the TOAD and pulled the tire gauge out of the glove box. He checked all the tires on the coach and the tires on the TOAD. They were all in good shape, so he put the gauge back in the car, and walked to the coach door. Jane was just starting to bring the slides in. Frank got into the driver's seat and started the engine.

"Hey, honey, go ahead and turn on the water pump after you're done there. Then I'll get the levelers up, and we can blow this burg."

"Why do we need the water pump on?"

"To feed the ice maker and the cold water dispenser," Frank said.

"Oh, yeah," Jane said. "Got to have that ice."

"Yep, may be a Martini night tonight," he replied, grinning back at her. She smirked and shook her head. Then Frank turned on the leveler console and hit the retract button. The coach lurched and settled down on its wheels, and you could hear the hydraulics pulling up the jacks to storage position.

"Alright, we're set, sweetie. Time to get belted in."

Jane came over and sat down. She put on her seat belt, and then Lucy came running over, looking up at her, tail wagging.

"Oh, alright," she said. "Come on up, girl." Lucy jumped up and settled on her lap.

Frank slowly pulled out of his spot, and turned onto the access road that led to the main gate. There were two coaches in front of them waiting to make the right turn onto the road, and as they sat there, Frank saw two more coaches come up in his rear view mirror.

"Mass exodus," Frank said. They got up to the gate, and saw Charlie and Chester sitting in chairs talking. They both got up when they saw Frank. They walked up to the window.

"Goodbye, Frank," said Charlie. "It was nice meeting you."

Same here," Chester said.

"It was a pleasure. We'll probably meet again," said Frank. "I didn't expect so many other folks to be leaving now."

"News hasn't been that great," Charlie said. "The C-17s won't be here. They had to be moved elsewhere. We're getting ready to leave too."

"Not surprised," Frank said. "What about your place?"

"You know, this place will keep," Charlie said. "I'll be back. It's not like they can burn the whole place down."

"True, this place may be a little more resistant to damage than a store or a motel," Frank said. "Is there a gas station open nearby?"

"Yes, you can't miss it, it's right on the way to Route 89," Charlie said.

"Great, thanks!" Frank said.

Jane leaned over and waved to the men. They waved back, and Frank got ready to leave.

"Goodbye and good luck," Frank said.

Frank made the right turn and followed the road towards the highway. He saw the gas station coming up fast. It was a truck stop, with great big lanes. There were several RVs there gassing up as he drove into the driveway.

"This is going to be expensive," Jane said. "Hope they still take plastic."

Frank parked the rig next to a pump, and shut off the engine. He got out of the coach, and went over to the propane tank. He turned the valve off. Then he walked up to the pump. He tried his credit card. It worked, and he selected Regular and pulled the fill nozzle out. He started fueling up. It didn't take that long....he still had almost three quarters of a tank. The pump shut off with a jolt, and Frank pulled the nozzle out and put it back on the pump. Then he closed the gas cap, and walked back to the pump. The receipt was waiting for him there. He grabbed it and got back in the coach.

"Not too bad," Frank said. "Only took 30 gallons."

Jane looked at the receipt and shook her head.

"Geez, $5.50 per gallon?"

"I actually expected it to be worse," Frank said. "We got topped off for about $170 bucks."

"Alright," Jane said, sounding exasperated. "Let's get out of here."

Frank nodded, and drove back onto the highway. The onramp for Route 89 was right there, and they got on, heading north. The road was nearly empty.

"Wonder why there aren't more people heading out of southern Arizona?" asked Jane. "This is a good way to go."

"Something probably has the road bottled up down there."

"Look, another military convoy," Jane said, pointing.

"Wow, look at all those tanks."

"Yeah, that's the most we've seen so far," Jane said. "It's a good sign."

"Or a bad sign. There aren't nearly as many personnel trucks with this one."

An explosion rumbled the ground under them.

"Whoa, did you hear that?" cried Jane. She had a worried look on her face. Lucy was looking all around, trying to figure out where the noise came from. She growled.

"Crap, somebody blew up one of the tanks. I can see it in my rear view mirror," Frank said. "Why don't you go look out the back window to see if there are any choppers around."

Jane got up, causing Lucy to jump to the floor. She made her way back and took a look out the window. No aircraft in sight. She came back up to her seat.

"Nothing flying back there that I can see. Boy am I glad we left when we did."

"You and me both," Frank said. "Wonder if it was an IED?"

They drove along, going to the east of the Grand Canyon. There were two more military convoys that raced past them, including one that had a crane on a giant trailer.

"I'll betcha that's being sent there to clean up the mess," Frank said. Jane nodded.

"It looks like about half of the coaches that were with us before are behind us again," Jane said, craning her neck to see back in the passenger side mirror.

"I know. I haven't seen the ones that were in front of us for a while. They probably got a ways ahead while we were pumping gas."

They were silent for a while, watching the scenery go by. It was peaceful, but both of them were nervous. It was heading towards dusk, causing the shadows of the trees to get longer and longer.

"Look, there's the Utah border!" said Jane.

"Finally," Frank said. "I don't see any checkpoints yet."

"If there are any, I would guess they would be on I-15, not this little highway."

"You may have a point there, Jane. Why don't you turn on the radio? It's been a while since we've heard news. Maybe there will be something on the battle down south."

"Alright," Jane said. She leaned over, turned on the radio and hit the seek button. Lucy jumped off her lap and got onto her bed. "Good, I needed a break from Miss Lucy."

"Yeah, I'm surprised she didn't pee on your lap when that explosion happened."

"Ahh, here's a news station," she said. She turned up the radio.

"News coming out of New York City is sketchy at best," said the announcer. "The incident happened just over an hour ago. All cities are now locking down their ports to incoming vessels, and searching anything already in their harbors."

Frank looked over at Jane, who had a terrified look on her face.

"Oh, crap, what happened?" he asked. Jane just shook her head.

"This just in," the announcer said. "Another device has gone off in Puget Sound, near Seattle, Washington. It appears to be a larger device than the one detonated in New York harbor."

No Safe Harbor

Jane had a horrified look on her face.

"Oh no, are they talking about what I think they're talking about?"

Frank glanced over at her, eyes wide open, shocked.

The radio announcer continued with the story.

"Seattle police are working out a way to evacuate as many people as possible. Prevailing winds will probably blow the fallout east, which is going to make evacuations more difficult."

"How close is Portland to Seattle?" Jane asked.

"Too close for comfort, but Sarah will probably be alright. The fallout is blowing to the east, and she's south."

"Should I try to call her?"

"Yes, but I'll bet you won't get through," Frank said. He felt numb.

Jane tried to call on her cell phone as the radio announcer continued.

"The blast in New York harbor has caused tremendous damage in lower Manhattan, Brooklyn, and Jersey City. There are no estimates of casualties there, but the numbers will be horrendous, as will the economic impact."

"I'm only getting a busy signal," Jane said.

"That's what I expected," Frank said. "I hope one of those doesn't go off in LA Harbor."

"Would Robbie live through that?"

"Probably, because he's on the other side of the hill from the harbor. I think the fallout would be going east, not north, but you never know."

"The White House has just released a statement," the announcer said. *"We know who made these attacks possible, and they will pay a heavy price."*

"We're getting close to Capitol Reef," Jane said. "See that sign we just passed? There's a big RV park just off of the highway up ahead, and several more down the road a ways"

"Good, I think we need to get off the road," Frank said. "I'm too worked up to drive."

"This just in," the announcer said. *"The Port of Vladivostok in Russia has just been hit. The device was larger than the New York bomb. It appears to have been the size of the device detonated earlier today in Puget Sound."*

"Crap," Frank said. "Well, at least this is good news in one way. I don't think there will be any nuke exchanges between Russia and the US, and they are the only country that is a real threat to our existence."

"Unless the Russians did that to themselves," Jane said.

"I wouldn't bet on that. They don't have enough ports as it is. They can't afford to blow one up."

"There's a good looking RV park about forty miles up the road, in Panguitch," Jane said, looking at her cellphone. "Think you can handle another forty miles?"

"Yeah, sure," Frank said.

"Ladies and gentlemen, we have yet another report of an attack, this time in Charleston Harbor," the announcer said. He sounded really shaken now.

"We are under a huge attack," Frank said. "This is really bad. The world will never be the same." He looked over at Jane. She was crying now.

"Can we turn that off for a while?"

"Sure, honey, go ahead," Frank said. Jane switched off the radio.

They were silent as the miles rolled by. They saw two military convoys going south, both with large numbers of tanks and artillery. The sun was slowly getting closer to the western horizon. Jane dosed off. Frank's mind was racing. Who did this? Obviously the Islamists were part of it, but who helped them? North Korea? Vladivostok was close to North Korea. Was China involved? How was our government going to respond?

Lucy got out of her bed and sat next to the passenger seat, whining to get Jane's attention. She wanted up.

"Lucy, quiet down," Frank whispered. Lucy turned her head to him, then turned back to Jane and whined some more. Jane finally stirred and woke up. She had a disoriented look on her face.

"How long was I out?" she asked.

"Not that long. Only about twenty minutes. I tried to get Lucy to quiet down."

"No problem, honey," she said. "Come on up, girl." Lucy jumped on her lap, and circled around a couple of times, then settled in.

"We're getting close to a town called Panguitch now, and I've been seeing signs about RV Parks there. I vote that we go to the first one that looks decent," Frank said.

"Alright with me."

The exit for the town was ahead of them, and Frank put on his turn signal. He looked in his rear view mirror saw the other coaches behind him do the same. He slowed down and took the turn into the town.

"Which way?" Frank asked.

"Turn right, and follow the road to the outskirts of town. There's a large park there. It's not very far."

The town looked almost deserted, until they passed a bar and grill about five blocks in. The parking lot was overflowing, and there were people outside the front door smoking. A couple of them waved to the caravan. They had sullen faces.

"There it is, Frank." Jane pointed to an access road on the right, next to a sign that said Capitol Paradise RV Park and Resort.

Frank pulled down the access road. There was a long parking and staging area next to the office. Frank pulled as far forward as he could, and shut off the engine.

"I'll go check it out," Frank said. He unhooked his seatbelt and headed for the door.

"I'll take Lucy out," Jane said. She got out of her seat, and reached for the leash.

Frank walked to the office door and opened it. Light flowed into the dusk. There was a middle aged woman at the counter. She had her hair up in a bun, and had a western style dress on.

"Good evening," she said. "I'm Hilda. Can I help you?" She was trying to smile, but Frank could tell that she had been crying.

"Do you have spaces with 50 amp?" Frank asked.

"Yes, we have plenty of space. This war has killed off all of our European tourist trade. How many in your party?"

"Well, we aren't exactly a party," Frank said. "We've just ended up leaving the last place we were in at the same time, and you can only go north at this point. I think there are twelve or thirteen coaches behind us. We were all down by the Grand Canyon earlier today."

The door opened, and Jeb walked in.

"Hi, Frank," he said.

"Jeb, good to see you. Glad we ended up in the same place."

"We have about ninety open spaces. Most are pull through," Hilda said. "Price is $40 per night. Is that alright?"

"Suits me," Frank said. "Still take credit cards?"

"Sure do," she said. "Just pick out a spot that you like, and come back later with the space number. We'll do the payment then," she said. "Any pets?"

"Just a small dog," Frank said.

"OK, that's fine, just clean up after it."

"Always," Frank said. "Should I tell the others to go on in?"

"No, I want them all to walk in here so I can get a look at them," Hilda said. "But you two can go ahead."

He smiled and walked out the door with Jeb.

"You been listening to the news?" Frank asked.

"No, why?"

"There have been nuke attacks in several of our harbors."

Jeb stopped walking, and looked Frank in the eyes.

"No," he said. "Where?"

"New York, Seattle, and Charleston," Frank said. "Maybe more by now. We turned off the radio a while ago."

"Who?"

"Don't know for sure. Pretty sure it isn't the Russians."

"Why?" asked Jeb.

"Somebody hit the port in Vladivostok too."

"Wow. Somebody is going to get it," Jeb said. They shook hands and walked back to their coaches as some of their fellow RVers were walking to the office.

"Well, what's the deal?" Jane asked, walking up with Lucy in tow.

"It's a little expensive, but they have plenty of spaces, and it's 50 amp. Forty bucks a night. We pick a space, and then go back to the office with the number."

"That isn't so bad," Jane said. Frank opened the door and Lucy bounded in. They followed.

Frank got in the driver's seat and started the engine. He pulled forward onto the access road, and into the park. The spaces were large, with nice shade trees. There was a pool and club house in the middle, and a few park model trailers towards the left that appeared to be occupied. Frank drove past the pool a little ways, and turned down a row of pull through sites to the left. He drove down close to the end of the row and pulled in.

"This looks long enough for the TOAD," Frank said. "Better get out and watch the tree branches for me, though."

Jane nodded and got up. She went out the door and looked up. There was plenty of clearance. She got in front of the coach and motioned Frank forward. He slowly pulled up until Jane put her hands up to stop him. She went around the back. The TOAD was out of the road, just barely. Frank was coming out of the door as she walked back towards it.

"You're good....the TOAD is out of the road. Nice space, actually."

"Good, I'll get her leveled out, and get the slides out."

Frank went back in and turned on the auto levelers and the whir of the hydraulic pumps sounded. The coach bounded and jerked its way to level. When it was done, Frank shut off the engine.

"Mr. Wonderful is on the bed, honey," Jane said from the bedroom. Frank walked to the console and pushed the button to extend the bedroom slide. Then he did the salon slides.

"I'll go get the hookups done," Frank said. He left the coach and went around to the back driver's side. He got the water and electric hooked up, and then brought out the sewer hose and connected that. "I'll need a shower tonight." he said to himself. He came around to the other side of the coach and unlocked the rear compartment. He pulled out the four chairs and the table. Jane came out the door and stopped on the steps.

"Shall extend the awning?" she asked.

"I wouldn't worry about it now. The sun is almost down."

"Alright. I turned off the water pump. Why don't you turn on the electric switch on the water heater? I think we are going to both need showers."

"I was already thinking that," Frank said. He chuckled. "I think I want a drink first, though, and I want to listen to the radio for a while."

"I'll bring the portable radio out there in a minute," Jane said. "What do you want to drink?"

"You know."

"OK, I'll make us martinis."

Frank nodded and smiled. He walked out to the road and looked down towards the clubhouse and pool. The other coaches were coming in and parking. There were more than he thought. Jeb's coach was in his row again, down towards the center access road. The lights inside the coach were already on, and he could see Jeb sitting at his dinette.

"Here's the drink, Frank," Jane said as she was walking down the steps. Lucy followed her, tail wagging.

"Great, thanks." He walked over to her, took his drink, and slipped his arm around her waist, pulling her close. He kissed her. She started to sob lightly.

"You alright?" he asked.

"Yes, sorry. Hard day. I still can't get to Sarah. Nothing but busy signals up there."

"It will settle down in a little while, probably." He took a sip out of his drink. "Oh, that is so good."

"I've got to go grab mine. I'll feed Lucy and Mr. Wonderful, and then be back out."

Frank nodded, and sat down. He had another sip of the drink, and tried to relax. He could hear the pitter patter of Lucy's feet as she followed Jane around in the coach. Dinner time always got her excited. Then he heard the cat meow. He laughed to himself, and shook his head. Nothing bothers Mr. Wonderful. He took another sip, bigger this time. He felt the gin hitting his brain. It was a good comfortable feeling. He heard the steps creak, and looked around to see Jane walking down. She shut the screen door behind her. She had the portable radio in her hand.

"Don't drink that too fast, sweetie," she said, sitting down. She put the radio on the table between their chairs. "You want me to turn this on now?"

"Let's wait for a few minutes and relax," he said.

Jane nodded, and took a sip of her drink.

They sat silently for a few minutes, looking at the scenery around them. Pine trees, green grass, gentle breeze. Cool air of dusk.

"You know, Frank, this place is really closer to Bryce than it is to Capitol Reef."

"Really? Might make it harder for some of the group to find us, then."

"It's on Hwy 89, and it's a good distance for a stop from where we came from, so I suspect we'll still see quite a few folks showing up here in the next day or so."

"Jeb is here already."

"Jeb?"

"Oh, sorry honey, I forgot. You didn't meet him. He was parked down at the start of the row we were on in Charlie's park. Nice guy."

"I recognize some of the other coaches from the last place too," Jane said.

They heard footsteps in the gravel, and looked over towards the road. It was Jeb.

"Hi, Jeb," Frank said, getting out of his chair. "This is my wife, Jane."

"Good to meet you, Jane," he said.

"Want a drink, Jeb?"

"No thanks, want a clear head tonight."

"Alright. Have a seat," Frank said, motioning to one of the empty chairs. They both sat down.

"Listened to the radio yet?" asked Jeb, looking down at it sitting on the table.

"No," Jane said. "We wanted to savor our drinks and relax for a few minutes."

"Well, quite a bit has happened."

"I figured that would be the case," Frank said.

"Our president and the president of Russia just made a joint statement. We are going to work together with them to take out the folks that did this, and everybody who helped them."

"Good," Frank said. "Did they say who did it?"

"No, they aren't saying anything official. The pundits are all over this, though, and I don't think it's going to be too hard to figure out as the events unfold."

"What are the pundits saying?" asked Jane.

"North Korea supplied the devices, and the usual suspects in the Middle East all had a hand in getting them placed and detonated. You know, Iran, Syria, Libya, what's left of Iraq, and Pakistan."

"All of these countries are denying it, of course…" Frank said.

"Of course, although Iran has been taunting. They are used to this milk-toast administration doing nothing. I think they will be sorry for that." He leaned back a little bit and stroked his beard.

"Any other of our cities hit?" asked Frank.

"We almost got hit in Baltimore's inner harbor. The FBI figured out where the device was and got to it before it could be detonated. They caught the people who were going to do the deed, too, but the media isn't saying anything about them. No names, no nationalities, nothing."

"Wow, that would have had an impact on Washington DC," Jane said.

"Oh, yeah, and some nutcase group has claimed that Venezuela has annexed Mexico," Jeb said. He laughed. "I suspect Venezuela will be a smoking hole sometime in the next 48 hours, and if anybody is going to annex Mexico, it will probably be us."

"Nothing from the Mexican government?" asked Frank.

"Well, a lot of bodies were found. The president, and half of their legislature, a bunch of judges, mayors, and police officials. Really nasty stuff. Beheadings and the like. But that news came out before the nuke attacks started, so not much is being said about Mexico anymore."

"Anything else?" Jane asked.

"Yeah. China moved a bunch of its army next to the border with North Korea. Russia warned them to get away from there. Lots of harsh words going back and forth."

"China doesn't want us to nuke North Korea," Frank said. "It's too close to them."

"That's what the pundits are saying."

"Is anybody making comments about China having something to do with this?"

"Not in the media, no," Jeb said. "But the internet is on fire with that. Lots of people saying that they are the only major power who has anything to gain from all of this."

"Oh oh," Jane said.

"Yeah, oh oh," Jeb said.

Frank finished his drink and set it down on the table.

"We better eat something before you drink another one of those," Jane said.

"I'm not going to have another. I'm calmed down enough now. I want to have a reasonably clear head."

"Good," Jane said.

Jeb got up out of his chair.

"I'll get out of your hair now," Jeb said. "Nice to know somebody here. Good talking to you."

"Same here," said Frank, standing up to shake hands. "Maybe Charlie and Chester will show up."

"Oh, you know those guys, do you?" Jeb asked, grinning.

"Well, not well, we only just met them. Chester was with us in Williams, and on the road up north. He was going to stick around at the last place until Charlie decided to leave."

"They left, I've already talked to them. They are coming here. I expect we'll see them in a couple of hours."

"Oh, so you know those guys too, huh," Frank said.

"Yeah, we go way back. I'll let you know when they show up."

"Great, thanks," Frank said as Jeb was walking away. He looked back and waved.

"Well, there you go," Frank said.

"Let's turn on the radio," Jane said. "I'm done just listening to other people telling me what happened."

"Good point," Frank said. He reached over and switched on the radio, and started searching for a news station. He found one pretty quickly.

"Russia has warned China to move its forces away from North Korean border within twenty four hours, or risk losing them," the announcer said. "China responded by asking for the UN to take up the matter tonight. The US government has said it will strike quickly, and has told China that it agrees with Russia and will not be deterred by China or the UN in this matter."

"Well, Jeb was right about that," Frank said. Jane nodded.

"The FBI is continuing to look at suspicious freighters in US harbors at this hour," the announcer said. "No official word yet on the identity of the people apprehended at the site of the Baltimore device. The president and key government officials have been moved to safe locations due to that incident."

"I wonder if there is anything in LA harbor?" Jane asked. I should call Robbie and see what he is hearing."

"Go ahead," Frank said. Jane got up and went into the coach to retrieve her phone, which she had put on the charger. She dialed Robbie's number as she was coming out. She sat down, phone at her ear.

"Robbie?" she asked.

"Mom, you got through. I've been trying to call you for a while now. It's nearly impossible to get a call to connect from here."

"Well, it's probably like when we have an earthquake," Jane said. "You know how they tell you to call a relative out of state?"

"Yeah, that's probably it," Robbie said.

"You've been watching the news, right?"

"Yes, all of the nuke attacks. Geez," Robbie said.

"Are they saying anything about LA Harbor?"

"Yes, they have been moving people out of the areas right around LA harbor, and Long Beach too. I hear that San Pedro is like a ghost town right now. And Wilmington, and Harbor city, and the western part of Long Beach."

"Do you think you are alright where you are?"

"I think so. We are a ways away from the big harbors. The closest thing to us is Marina Del Rey, and there aren't any large ships in there."

"Good," Jane said.

"Oh crap," Robbie said. "Big flash to the north….."

{ 3 }

Special Bulletin

There was static on the line, and it disconnected.

"Oh, no," Jane cried.

"We don't know what happened yet, honey. Don't jump to any conclusions. Those flashes can be seen for a long distance," Frank said.

"It's our little boy," Jane said, sobbing. That was too much for Frank. He broke down and cried too. He got up and hugged Jane.

"If it wasn't real close like Marina Del Rey, he's probably going to be OK, honey. The wind is going to blow the fallout to the east," Frank said, looking at her face almost nose to nose, holding her head. She stared at him with wet red eyes.

"It will be on the radio soon. Let's turn it up," Jane said.

Frank nodded and turned up the radio. It was on a commercial.

"Maybe we ought to have another drink," Jane said.

"No," Frank replied. He pulled his chair right next to Jane's and sat down, putting his arm around her shoulder as they listened to the radio.

The commercials were over. The announcer came back on.

"We have received a statement from the White House that retaliation has started, and will be working its way from the closest perpetrators outward. Venezuela has just been rocked by nuclear attacks in all of its ports and all of its major population centers."

"Good," Frank said. Jane looked at him and nodded.

"This just in. A small device was just detonated in Southern California, in Ventura Harbor. This is a harbor that was not considered a threat, so now all of the municipalities with small harbors are on alert, and are searching all boats."

"Oh, thank God," Jane said. "He's going to be alright."

"Yes," Frank said. He petted her head and her cheek, as she started to calm down.

"The Cities of Ventura and Oxnard have sustained large loss of life and catastrophic damage. The prevailing wind is to the east, which will cause problems for the rich agricultural area that lies in that direction. Authorities have said they will require evacuation of people as far east as Simi Valley due to the fallout danger. There are also plans to evacuate the nearby communities of Thousand Oaks and Agoura. At this time it appears that the nearest big population areas up and down the coast will survive and not need evacuation. These communities include Santa Barbara to the north and the cities along Santa Monica Bay to the south."

"There it is," Jane said. "He's going to be alright."

"I hope they do a good job searching Marina Del Rey and King Harbor." Jane looked at him, worried.

"Do you think he's still in danger?"

"Possibly," Frank said. "Nothing we can do about it, though."

"In other news," the announcer continued, "Russia has started using the same strategy in their country to take out the radical Islamists, which is to take out the closest bases first, and then expand outward. They have chosen not to use nuclear weapons nearby their country. They are using a scorched earth eradication in areas of their country that are linked to the device in Vladivostok. At the current hour, they have leveled all mosques in Chechnya, and are searching house to house for Islamist leaders in that province. The UN and Amnesty International are already protesting the actions."

"Interesting. Wonder if there are protests for what we have done in Venezuela. Seems to me that is worse," Jane said.

"We probably are getting protests, but Venezuela's government was an active participant, and they committed an act of war much worse than Japan did in 1941."

"Breaking news," the announcer said. "A device has been located in the San Francisco Bay area, on a large private yacht. There is a manhunt going on right now to find the perpetrators. The owners of the yacht were found below deck. All of them were murdered."

"Wow," Frank said. "That's probably what they did in Ventura. It's going to be hard to find all of them. There are thousands and thousands of private boats along all of our coasts."

"The White House has announced a press conference for 9:00 PM EST tonight," the announcer said. "And it is expected that the Russian president will join him for part of the briefing."

Frank and Jane heard footsteps in the gravel, and looked towards the road. It was Charlie and Chester.

"Hi, Frank. Hi, Jane," said Chester. Charlie was standing next to him smiling.

"Well well well, I suspected we'd be seeing you guys again, Frank said, standing up. He walked over to them and shook hands. Jane followed him, nodding and smiling at the two men.

"You want to sit down?" asked Jane. "We've been listening to the radio."

"We've got a better suggestion. The clubhouse is set up with two flat screen TVs, and we brought as much food as we could carry from my park," Charlie said. "Why don't you folks join us? We have CNN on one screen and Fox News on the other.....on opposite sides of the room, so you can choose your poison."

"Actually, that sounds great," Frank said. "What do you think, honey?"

"I'm good with it, but I want to try to reach Robbie one more time," she said.

"Good idea," Frank said. "Alright, we'll be along in a little bit. Thanks!"

Chester and Charlie nodded, and then turned to leave. Frank and Jane sat back down. Jane dialed Robbie's number on her cell phone and put it to her ear. She gave Frank a thumbs up, because it started ringing instead of giving her a busy signal.

"Put it on speaker," Frank said. "Jane nodded and pulled the phone from her ear. She pushed the speaker button and put the phone on the table.

"It's ringing a long time," Frank said.

"He probably just stepped away from the phone for a few minutes."

There was a click.

"Mom," Robbie said.

"Yes, honey, it's your father and me. I've got you on speaker."

"I've been trying to call you, but still can't connect from here," Robbie said. "You heard about what happened in Ventura?"

"Yes, son," Jane said.

"We were afraid it happened in Del Rey," Frank said.

"I'd be toast if that happened. They have pretty large crews looking through the boats in Redondo Harbor and Marina Del Rey. Also down south in all of the pleasure boat harbors. You heard about the yacht up in Frisco, right?"

"Yes, we've had the news on the radio," Jane said. "We are going to go over to the clubhouse in a few minutes. They have a couple of big screens with CNN and Fox News on over there."

"And a bunch of food too," Frank added. "How are your supplies holding up there?"

"We're in good shape, dad. We still haven't gotten through even half of the food we had here, and now we can go to the stores, as long as it's not past curfew. Some items are getting hard to find though. Fresh produce, for example."

"I'm not surprised," Frank said. "It takes constant truck traffic to keep SoCal stocked with produce, and the roads just aren't what they were. There's still a war going on in the Southwest."

"Wow!" Robbie exclaimed. "A nuke just went off in Paris. They just put pictures up."

"Oh no, Paris too?" Jane said. She was starting to cry again. "When is this going to stop?"

"It just got announced on the Radio," Frank said. "Listen."

"Robbie, we gotta go," Jane said. "Take care of yourself. Love you."

"Love you too, mom, and you too dad," Robbie said.

"Love you, son. Be careful," Frank said. Jane pushed the button on the phone to end the call.

Frank turned up the radio.

"The device was probably in a boat on the Seine river," the announcer said. "This is the worst attack yet. It happened in a very densely populated area. This one is going to have a death toll in the million range."

"No," said Jane. Frank was unable to say anything. He just sat, staring at the radio.

"Frank, let's go to the clubhouse," Jane said. Frank nodded. They put Lucy in the coach and closed the door. Frank locked it up, and they walked silently to the center of the park. Light was flooding out of the windows at the clubhouse. A few people were standing outside on the veranda, smoking. They all nodded when Frank and Jane climbed the steps. One of them said "Hi Frank." Frank nodded.

They entered the large room. There was a big screen TV by the door, on the wall to the right. Across the room was another TV. There were people huddled around both of them, most having plates of food. To the left of the door, along the wall, was a long table with lots of food. Frank and Jane walked over to that, and each of them loaded up a plate. They walked over to the TV on the side of the room away from the door, and pulled up chairs. It was on CNN. There were pictures of the devastation in Paris on the screen. No commentary at the moment, just video. The bottom of the screen had headlines flowing by, and the CNN logo was at the bottom right side of the screen. Several people watching had tears in their eyes.

Charlie walked up to Frank and Jane. He was standing next to Hilda. They both smiled.

"So this is the famous Frank and Jane?" asked Hilda.

"Yep," Charlie said with a grin.

"We aren't famous," Frank said. Jane looked over at Frank and smirked.

"You two look like you know each other," Jane said to Charlie and Hilda.

"Yes, we go back a ways," Hilda said. "I used to date this old troublemaker way back when."

"Then she came to her senses," Charlie said, laughing.

"No, then you met the real love of your life and got married," said Hilda. "But that's good. I had a love of my life too. He left me two years ago. Cancer got him."

"So sorry to hear that, Hilda," Frank said. "So I suppose you know Chester too?"

Hilda got a grin on her face.

"Another old reprobate that I dated when I was young and stupid."

"Yeah, but you almost married him," Charlie said.

"True. That would have been interesting," she said, smirking.

"Really," Jane said. "So this really is old home week for you guys."

"Oh, we see each other pretty often, actually," Hilda said.

The commentators came back on the screen. It was a young woman and an older man. They both looked exhausted.

"We have received a video from an Islamist leader in Iraq," said the male commentator. "It arrived on YouTube less than half an hour ago."

"We bring it to you now, uncut," the woman said.

The video displayed on the screen. There was an old man in a white robe, with a long beard and a round hat. He was sitting on a rug. On either side of him stood younger men with long beards, dressed in black, holding automatic weapons. Behind them was the logo of the terror organization that had recently taken over a large chunk of both Syria and Iraq.

The old man started to speak, his lips starting to move with no sound coming out. Then an English translator started to speak.

"By the grace of Allah, I am here to announce a new Caliphate. We have taken the battle to the Infidel in every corner of the western world, and we have just begun. Truly all praise belongs to Allah. We and our partners have placed agents in every corner of your free societies, and will use your own laws to bring you under the control of the Allah and Muhammad (peace and blessings be upon him) His slave and Messenger. I have been declared the new Caliph of the global Islamic State."

"Hey, spinach chin, stuff it," yelled a man behind them. Somebody asked him to be quiet.

The Caliph continued.

"The peoples of the world will agree that they will submit to Allah, or accept dhimmi status."

"What's dhimmi status?" asked Charlie.

"I'll tell you after this idiot is done talking," Frank whispered.

"The attacks will not stop, as you are not yet convinced that you cannot defeat Allah and his armies.....Allah willing, and nothing is too great for Allah."

"Turn this jackass off," shouted somebody from the other side of the room.

The video ended abruptly.

"It looked like the end of that was missing," Jane said.

The commentators came back on the screen.

"We now take you to the White House," the woman commentator said.

The screen displayed a briefing room with an empty podium. The presidential seal was on the front of it, and there were flags on either side.

"Hey, that's not the White House," said somebody over to the right.

"Right, they are operating from a secure location," somebody said. "I'm surprised the CNN commentator didn't mention that."

Frank turned around to see who said that. It was Jeb, standing behind him about ten feet away. He nodded, and Jeb nodded in return.

"So what is dhimmi status?" Charlie asked again.

"Oh yeah, sorry," Frank said. "It's a status that Muslim countries place Christians and Jews into. It is supposed to allow you to live and practice your religion freely, but you have to pay a special tax that Muslims don't have to pay, and there are a lot of restrictions. You don't have the same rights as a Muslim in court, for example. But they aren't supposed to kill you, since you are also considered 'children of the book' and retain some protection."

"What about athiests?" asked Chester, who was walking up.

"I don't think that is considered 'protected' by these folks," Frank said.

"Well, they will have to kill me because I'm not putting up with this crap, not for one minute," Charlie said, his face turning red.

Jeb started laughing, and walked up.

"They ain't gonna win, Charlie," he said. "These fools can't even pump and refine their own oil without help from western companies.

They arc good at breaking things, but that's about as far as it goes. We'll go through them like shit through a goose if it's a real fight."

"Hey, here comes the President," said somebody.

The screen showed him walking up to the podium. He had a somber look on his face.

"Good evening, ladies and gentlemen. I won't recount what has happened over the last twenty four hours, as I'm sure all of you have been following the news. The United States, the EU, and the Russian Federation are cooperating on a level not seen since the Second World War to settle this matter and bring the guilty parties to justice. And make no mistake, our response will not be a restrained series of police actions. These attacks are acts of war, and will be treated as such. We will use our most terrible weapons, and fight as if our very survival is at stake, because it is."

There was applause in the clubhouse, and in the press room.

"A few words about moderate Muslims," the president continued. "There is no cause and no excuse to punish the moderate Muslims due to the actions of these radicals. Remember that moderate Muslims living in our cities have been killed in these attacks, right alongside people of every other faith. That being said, the United States is not going to have the resources to protect all of you at all times from angry citizens. I suggest that you keep a low profile while we concern ourselves with winning this war."

"Finally, a few words about Martial Law. We have put that in place only in areas that are under attack, and we will not leave it in place for long. I know there are many out there who are concerned about the guarantees of Liberty which reside in our Constitution and Bill of Rights. This Administration takes those guarantees very seriously. Martial Law will only be declared when we need it to fight the enemy. Rumors of an extension of Martial Law to all areas of the United States are false. We have no reason to do that. We will not do that. I hope that puts these fears to rest. That is all for now, and sorry, but I won't take any questions at this time." He left the podium and walked off to the right.

"You know, I'm actually proud of this president for once," Frank said. Jane looked at him and smiled.

"You aren't going to believe this Frank, but I'm worried about some of what he said," Jane said.

"What, I can't agree with your guy and be on your side of this?" he asked, laughing.

"He just declared open season on Muslims in the United States."

"Oh, you think I didn't catch that?" Frank asked. "I understand exactly what he is doing, and I think it's brilliant."

"Please explain."

"Well, you heard old spinach chin saying they were going to use our society's laws against us, correct?"

"Yes."

"Those comments by the president just made that tactic null and void," Frank said.

"I agree," Jeb said, walking up behind them. "The Caliph, may he bathe in pig blood, is thinking that our government will protect Muslims when the bad element in that community starts holding demonstrations and pushing people around, like they've been doing in Europe for the last ten years or so. They try that here and the bubbas among us are going to take them apart, with no interference from the government. The commander in chief just locked down the sleeper cells. He applied a kind of Martial Law, but only on the bad guys."

"Don't you think this could get out of hand?" asked Jane.

"Oh, it will get out of hand, at first," Jeb said. "It won't take to many incidents to drive these folks underground and out of action."

"Oh, crap, look," Frank said, pointing to the TV screen. There was video on the screen of a part of London on fire.

"Not London," said Jane. "Please, not London."

The commentator came back on the screen.

"That amazing footage was taken in Westminster. About an hour ago, the British Secret Service foiled a nuclear attack on the city. It was another pleasure craft, on the Thames River. The device was disarmed and all suspects were apprehended. According to BBC they were of Pakistani and Syrian nationality."

"They stopped the plot, so what's with the fires?" asked Jane.

The announcer continued.

"As you can see, we have fires burning in the background. At the time that the news about the foiled nuclear attack was released, Islamic demonstrators were still camped outside Westminster Abbey. Men flooded out of the nearby pubs, beat most of the demonstrators to death, and burned their tents, signs, and other items. London police looked on, but took no action."

"Looks like the Prime Minister and our President are on the same page," Jeb said. "Bravo!"

The screen now went to another special bulletin. The tired commentators were back on, looking at papers on their desk. They both looked really tired.

"Ladies and Gentlemen, we have two more major stories to report. First, the United States Government has announced that it is moving in to Mexico to take control of that country, in lieu of an official Mexican government. The agents from Venezuela who had attempted to take over have fled that country after Mexican nationals stormed the palace. The United States is coming in at the request of what is left of the Mexican government. They will not answer questions about the length of our occupation or plans for the future."

"I was expecting this," Frank said. "We're going to annex Mexico. Wait and see." Jane looked at him and shook her head.

"The second story comes out of North and South Korea. United States and South Korean troops are evacuating from border next to the de-militarized zone, at the same time that the Chinese are pulling their troops away from the northern border of North Korea. It is widely expected that a major attack is imminent, and sources say that North Korea is getting ready to fire their ICMBs in desperation. South Korea and Japan are trying to protect their people as best they can, and missile defense units are at the ready. Although untested, North Korean ICMBs do have the capability to hit the western United States as well as the Russian Federation and other Asian countries."

{ 4 }

TV Night

Everybody in the room was silent, staring at the TV screens, listening to the pundits discuss the threat from North Korea. Then a man in the middle of the room broke the silence.

"C'mon, folks, the North Korean ICBMs can't get to us. We're too far inland."

"Some of us have family on the west coast," shouted a woman close to where Frank and Jane were sitting.

Jane stood up.

"Yes, both of our kids are on the west coast," Jane said.

"One of mine is in Hawaii," said another person.

"My son is stationed in South Korea," said another woman. She was crying. That hushed the crowd. Another woman walked over and hugged her.

"Well, folks, I suggest we try to calm ourselves down," Hilda said, standing up.

"I agree," Jeb said, also standing up. "There's nothing we can do about this now, and besides, those idiots running North Korea have failures more often than success with their longer range weapons. Most of these things are going to fall into the ocean."

"The operative word is 'most', my friend," said Chester. "But you're right, there isn't a thing we can do other than watch and wait."

Jane looked down on her lap. Her phone was buzzing. It was Sarah's number. She quickly put the phone to her ear, and looked Frank in the eye. She mouthed 'Sarah'.

"Mom?" a scared voice said.

"Yes, honey," she replied. Her brow got furrowed. Frank saw that and it made him uneasy.

"We were just told to evacuate Portland," Sarah said. "Mom, I'm scared."

"Don't be scared, honey, just leave. Now. As fast as you can. Don't worry about your stuff."

"What about Franklin?" she asked. She was crying now.

"You have a cat carrier, don't you?"

"Yes," she said.

"Put Franklin in there and throw him in the back seat," Jane said. "But leave now."

"Where are you guys?" she asked.

"We are in southern Utah. Go east, and then call us. Don't go south of Utah."

Frank nodded at Jane, and put his hand out for the phone.

"Your father wants to talk to you," Jane said. She handed the phone to Frank.

"Hi, sweet pea, how are you holding up?"

"I'm scared, daddy," she said. Frank got tears in his eyes. He used his free hand to wipe them away.

"Listen, honey," he said. "You need to leave right now. There is going to be a lot of traffic on the road, but just head to the east as fast as you can. Do you have anybody who can go with you?"

"My roommate," she said. "She's pushing me to get going too."

"Good," Frank said. "Leave now. You can join us in the motorhome when you get out here."

"Alright, daddy, I'm leaving now. I love you."

"Love you too, honey. Be careful," Frank said. He handed the phone back to Jane.

"You're going to go?" asked Jane.

"Yes, mom, we're leaving right now. I'm taking the cat too."

"Good. Take care. I love you sweetie."

"Mom?"

"Yes, dear," Jane said.

"What about Robbie?"

"We don't know, but we'll try to call him. LA is a long way south, he might not be in the same danger you are in," Jane said. "But don't worry about it, just go."

"Alright. Love you, mom," she said. She hung up the phone.

Frank looked at Jane. She was on the verge of tears, but she also had a look of relief on her face.

"You alright?" Frank asked.

"I'm glad she called, and I'm glad she's leaving. Do you think Robbie is in danger?"

"I don't know. Certainly less danger than Sarah would be in if the North Korean ICBMs actually work."

"Hey, look at the screen. They are talking about North Korean missile capabilities now," Jeb said. Everybody quieted down and turned to the screen.

The commentator was standing in front of a graphic of the Pacific Rim, which had circles showing the ranges of their different missiles. Some people in the room reacted with a gasp.

"As you can see, the longest range missile is technically capable of reaching into the US Mainland," the commentator said. *"The name of this missile is the Taepodong-2. There is much disagreement on the range of this missile. With extra boosters, this missile would be technically capable of hitting as far into the US mainland as the Rocky Mountains. Our best experts do not believe that. They say the real range of the rocket much smaller. They say this missile is not capable*

of hitting the lower 48 states of the US at all, but it is capable of hitting the western part of Alaska, and possibly the Hawaiian Islands."

"Crap," said Jane. "I don't know if I trust our intelligence enough to stake my life on it."

The commentator continued.

"One thing to bear in mind, though, is the reliability of these weapons. The Taepodong-2 has been tested three times. Once in July 2006, once in April 2009, and once in April 2012. All three tests failed. The real danger is the Rodong missile, which is operational and fairly reliable. It has a range of just 1,300 km. That puts most of Japan in range, and of course South Korea and parts of China and Russia."

Jane looked over at Frank.

"I'm going to try to call Robbie," she said.

"Alright, but don't tell him to come here. I think he's in more danger on the road between here and there than he is from the North Koreans."

"Agreed," Jane said. She dialed the phone, but shook her head. "Busy signal."

"I'm surprised Sarah got through."

The commentator put a new map up, that centered on the Middle East, showing rings of missile ranges.

"It is believed that North Korea has been selling its missiles to Iran and other nations in the Middle East, but so far we can only verify that they have sold the Scud-B, with a range of 300 km, and the Scud-C with a range of 500 km. Neither of those systems is capable of going very far. They would not even reach Israel. There are unconfirmed reports of the Taepodong–1 and Taepodong-2 missiles being sold to Iran, but even if that is true, there is still the issue of test failures for both of these systems. If Iran did possess the Taepodong-2 missile, technically they would be able to target areas as far away as

Greenland to the north, most of the African continent, India, and large sections of China, Southeast Asia, and the Russian Federation."

"That puts all of Europe squarely in the crosshairs," Jeb said dryly. "Maybe they are re-thinking some of the sanctions we asked them to help with."

"Again, I must stress that there have been no successful tests of either class of Taepodong missile," the commentator said. *"The biggest threat that North Korea poses is to South Korea, Japan, and the thousands of American soldiers that are in the area."*

"The lines are still busy into LA," Jane said. *"We probably aren't going to get to him tonight."*

Frank nodded.

Jeb walked over, with Charlie and Chester.

"You know what we've noticed?" asked Charlie. "Nobody is talking about what is going on in the Southwest."

"I was wondering about that myself," Frank replied. "It would be nice to know if we have to evacuate here in the near term." Jane looked over at Frank and nodded.

"Hey, Hilda, can you get any of the local TV channels here?" Jeb asked.

"Sure, we have the usual CBS, NBC, and ABC affiliates. Why?"

"We are wondering what is going down south," Charlie said.

"Worried about your Park?" asked Hilda.

"Well, yes, but I'm more worried about us," he replied. "If they've taken advantage of the confusion of all of these nuke attacks, they might have moved through northern Arizona. They could be on their way here, you know. They probably can't go south anymore."

"If they were smart, they would surrender," Chester said. "They're stranded with no place to go."

Frank laughed. Everybody looked over at him.

"What's so funny?" asked Hilda.

"Those people are out-of-their-minds crazy. They want to die. You've seen how they act. They aren't going to surrender. Our military or our citizens are going to have to take them out."

"He's right," Jeb said. "Of course the Texicans might chase them down and kill them all. They did a good job of kicking them out of their state."

"True, but Texas has a long border to protect, and the enemy might still be coming in from Mexico," Chester said. "If the bad guys in Arizona are far enough to the west now, they might decide to let Arizona and Utah take care of their own problems."

"We saw several more military caravans going south as we were driving here," Jane said. "Lots of tanks and artillery."

"True, I don't think the battle is over just because of these nuke attacks," Chester said.

Jane looked over at Hilda.

"Let's turn it to the local channel for a few minutes. CNN is starting to repeat now anyway."

Hilda nodded, and walked over to a cabinet under the TV screen, opened a drawer, and pulled out the remote. She changed the channel.

There was a local newscast on, with video of people stripping local grocery stores clean in a frenzy.

"This video is from Flagstaff, earlier today," the announcer said. *"People are stocking up and hunkering down. It's reminiscent of what happens when a hurricane is on the way. There has been intense fighting east and south of the city. Enemy forces are stronger than expected, and are fighting desperately at this hour. The Army is bringing in troops, but not fast enough to end the battle. There are also battles going on to regain Tucson and Phoenix, and that is a drain on resources. The Texas forces have retreated back across their own border now, and are working to stop the influx of enemy fighters coming from the south. It is expected that the flow of terrorists will*

stop, as the US forces link up with what is left of the Mexican military and shut off all of the supply and entry routes in that country."

"This isn't giving me a warm fuzzy feeling," Charlie said. "It sounds to be like we haven't even been able to shut off the influx of enemy from Mexico. We are spread way too thin."

Jeb nodded, and so did Frank.

"Well," Jeb said, "if we lose Flagstaff, we will want to go further north, I recon."

"Yes," Frank said.

Hilda had a terrified look on her face. Charlie saw it.

"I know, Hilda, it's hard to leave what you've worked for all of your life behind, but trust me, it's better than getting killed over it."

"I know what you've just gone through," she replied, tears running down her cheeks.

"There's still a good chance that they won't come this way, you know," Frank said. "They probably aren't going to focus on taking new territory at this point. They have to know they are not going to win."

"You'd think so, but we know how these folks are," Jeb said. "We might have to defend ourselves, you know."

Jane got a worried look on her face.

"What?" asked Frank.

"The enemy is going to need to find out where they can get supplies when they run low. They might send scouting and raiding parties up here."

"You know, she's right," Jeb said. "We'd better get ready to watch for them. We need to find out how many people here are armed, and what their experience is. We might have to post sentries."

"Or just take off and go further north," Jane said.

"Let's not get too excited yet, folks," Chester said. "But we need to keep an eye out."

"How secure is the park, Hilda?" asked Jeb.

"Actually, it's more secure than you'd think," Hilda said. "We have chain link fence with razor wire along the top all the way around the back of the property, and I can close up the front too. Jerry insisted on doing that back about 8 years ago."

"Jerry?" Frank asked.

"My late husband," she replied. "Anyway, he decided to put up the fencing because of deer coming in here and chewing up all the flowers. The razor wire came later, because of two incidents with cougars that we had during that last big drought. I was against it at the time, but now I'm glad we did it."

"I'm surprised," Jane said. "I didn't notice anything."

"Oh, it's a ways back there," Jane said. "I insisted on that. You don't want to feel like you are in a POW camp during vacation. It's back far enough that it's hard to see from the camping spaces."

"Are those hunting blinds that Jerry used to brag about still back there?" asked Chester.

"Well, I never took them down," Hilda said. "But I don't know what kind of shape they are in. Things built in trees don't tend to last very long. They are outside the fencing, but they do have a good view of the area."

"Good," Jeb said. "I suggest we take a look at the fencing, the blinds, and the general topography tomorrow morning."

"I second that," Charlie said.

"Alright, I'm with you," Frank said. Jane nodded approval, but she looked worried.

"Are you just about ready to go back to the coach, Frank?"

"Yes, I'm getting tired, and Miss Lucy probably is ready for a walk, too."

"Looks like this party is starting to break up anyway," Jane said. She nodded towards the door, where people were slowly starting to filter out. They both got up, and said goodnight to Charlie, Hilda, Jeb, and Chester. Then they walked to the door, and out into the soft warm night air.

"We may have to turn on the air conditioner tonight," Jane said.

"Yeah, it's definitely getting warmer. It's nice, though," Frank said. "I love this country."

"Me too. Wish we were just on vacation."

"Well, we should try to enjoy it as much as we can, regardless," Frank said. He put his arm around her and pulled her close as they walked.

"I hope things go well on the road for Sarah," Jane said.

"Me too," Frank said. "Sounds like Lucy can hear us."

Jane could barely hear the dog starting to bark.

"Where did you get such good ears?" she asked.

"Don't know. You want me to take her out?"

"I'll go too," Jane said. Frank unlocked the door, and Lucy jumped out, tail wagging furiously. Mr. Wonderful approached the door.

"Oh oh, watch the door, Frank."

"I see him. I'm going to go in and turn on the air conditioners. It's a little warm in there." He climbed in the door. The hum of the air conditioners started up. Frank came back out, holding the dog leash and poop bags.

Frank handed the leash to Jane and she hooked it up to Lucy while he closed and locked the door. Then they started a leisurely walk, guided by Lucy as usual.

"What are you thinking, Frank?"

"About what?"

"Should we stick around here and help defend this place, or should we get the heck out of here?"

"I don't know. What do you think, honey?"

Jane looked at him as they walked. He was scanning the area around the path they were on.

"You are already on watch," Jane said.

"Can't help it."

"Stress isn't good for people our age."

"I know, Jane. Either is guilt."

"You'd feel guilty if we leave?"

"I don't know. Maybe."

"Why? We didn't sign up for anything."

"I know that. If I was one hundred percent sure we would be safer on the road than we would be here, I'd be planning to leave tomorrow morning."

"Something worries you about being on the road?"

"No, Jane, something worries me about being on the road by ourselves."

Jane looked at him in the eye, trying to understand what he was thinking. She shook her head.

"I guess I don't understand," she said.

"If we stay here, we may run the risk of having to fight off a raiding party, but we can prepare and have a pretty good chance of successfully defeating them, if the topography lends itself to that. There's obviously game here that we can hunt, and water, and other supplies. Not enough to last forever, but probably enough to last for quite a few weeks. If we are out on the road, we are on our own. And we aren't twenty five anymore."

"True, we aren't twenty five anymore. I sense that you're worried about more than the enemy."

"Yes, I am. Food is going to start to get scarce. So are things like clean water and batteries and gasoline and motor homes. We may run into scavengers. In fact, we probably will run into them, or worse. We don't want to be alone if that happens."

"So you think it's better to stand and fight?"

"Depends on what you mean. If the whole Islamic army is on its way here, we obviously have to leave as quickly as we can, but then all of us would be leaving together. If we have scouting parties showing up, we'd probably be better off to stay here and help the group take them on, if leaving here would mean leaving by ourselves."

"Alright, I get it, and I think I'm agreeing with you," Jane said. "After we check out the area tomorrow, we should have a meeting with the whole group to discuss all of this, figure out what we have in the way of supplies, arms, and resources, and do some planning."

"There's the Jane I know and love."

She smiled at Frank and grabbed his hand. They entwined their fingers like high school kids, and continued to walk silently for a little while. They could see people slowly streaming out of the clubhouse, and they could see the lights in coaches coming on all over the park as people got home.

"It's amazing how quickly Lucy learned to recognize our coach," Frank said. "Look at her. She wants to go home, and she's trying to drag us right over there."

"She's a smart one."

They got to the coach. Frank handed the leash to Jane and unlocked the door. He pulled it open, being careful to watch for Mr. Wonderful. When he got the screen door open, Lucy jumped quickly up the steps. Jane followed her in, and then Frank. He shut the door behind him. It was nice and cool in the coach now.

"You want a snack or a drink or something, Frank?"

"No thanks, honey. I just want to settle in, and turn on the TV to see if anything else is going on."

"Alright," she said, turning on a couple of lights in the salon. Frank went into the bedroom and changed into some gym shorts and a tee-shirt. He came back out and sat on the couch. Jane was at the fridge, getting a glass of ice water.

"Want one?" she asked.

"Yes, that sounds good, thanks," Frank said. He picked up the TV remote and turned it on. He didn't have the cable hooked up yet, so he couldn't get to CNN or Fox News. He searched for a local channel that had a decent signal. He found one of the network affiliates, which was showing a cop drama.

"This OK for a few minutes?" he asked. "The news is coming on at 11:00."

"Sure. I'm going to go get into my nightgown." She walked into the bedroom and slid the door shut.

Suddenly the cop show stopped, and there was a Special Bulletin graphic on the screen. Then the network anchor was on.

"We have developments in North Korea at this hour. This is a video feed, being shown live. Look over to the right hand corner of the screen. There is an ICMB on the launch pad being fueled."

"Oh oh, here it starts," Frank said as Jane walked out in her nightgown and robe.

"What? Jane asked, getting a concerned look on her face.

"Look, there's live video of the North Koreans getting one of their ICBMs loaded with fuel."

"No. Not already!"

{ 5 }

Watch the Perimeter

J ane sat down next to Frank on the couch, looking at the image of the ICBM with steam coming out around it. She was trembling.

"Wonder who's taking this video feed?" asked Frank

"This is too soon," Jane said. "Sarah is probably sitting on the freeway in creeping traffic right now. She might still be in the city center."

"If we've got video like that, chances are pretty good that the Air Force already knows where this is."

Suddenly there was a bright flash on the screen, and then the video feed went dead.

"We just got it," Frank said. "Probably one of our stealth bombers. I'll bet they've been cruising around that area for the last day or so."

The commentator was back on the screen.

"Although we don't have confirmation yet, it appears that we have taken out that missile facility. We also have unconfirmed reports that there are other attacks happening against North Korea right now."

Frank could hear people cheering around the park.

"Guess everybody is watching TV," Frank said.

"I feel like cheering myself," Jane said. There were still tears running down her cheeks, but she had a smile on her face.

"Well, hopefully they got to all of the launching pads before anything was launched," Frank said. "Maybe I'll have a drink now. I'm not getting to sleep right away, that's for sure. You want one?"

"Sure."

Frank got up and went over to the kitchen counter. He got out the Gin and Vermouth, and started working on martinis. Lucy jumped up onto the warm spot that Frank left on the couch and settled in next to Jane. She rested her head on Jane's lap and sighed. Jane looked down at her and petted her head.

"I'm going to try Robbie again," she said.

"Good idea," Frank said. "It's not too late, plus they are an hour behind us."

"It's ringing," Jane said.

There was a click on the line.

"Hi, Mom. Did you see us take out that ICBM? That was awesome."

"Yes, dear, we have the TV on too. How are things there? How are you doing?"

"It's been crazy here. Lots of people trying to go east. The Army is letting people through, but the traffic is a mess, and we can't go straight east or south east because of the enemy positions in southern Arizona and Nevada. That takes away a lot of the better roads. You have to head more to the north."

"Sarah was told to evacuate from Portland. She's heading towards us now."

"They might be stopping the evacuations," Robbie said. "Just heard that on CNN. Sounds like we took out all of the North Korean missile sites before they even knew we were coming."

"Good. What are you going to do?"

"I don't know yet. I talked to my supervisor. He said it would be a couple of weeks before work starts up again, so I think we are just going to hang out for a while."

"Alright, son. I won't keep you. I know it's late. Take care of yourself."

"You too, mom. Love you."

"Love you too, Robbie." She took the phone from her ear and ended the call.

"How is he?" asked Frank, as he handed her a martini.

"He's good. He doesn't even sound worried anymore. He just sounds bored."

"Good. I'm going to throw on my robe and see if I can get the cable TV connection working."

"Alright, honey." She took a sip of the martini. "Mmmmm, this tastes good."

"Drink up, and maybe I'll get another chance at you," he said, grinning, while he walked into the bedroom to get his robe.

"You just might at that," she said with a giggle.

Frank walked to the door of the coach, pulling on his robe. He took another big swallow of his drink, and then set it on the kitchen counter. He picked up a flashlight out of the cabinet right by the door and went outside. He walked around to the back of the coach, and opened up the electrical compartment. Then he picked up the coax cable that was coiled up next to the power pedestal and ran it up through the hole in the bottom of the electrical compartment. He screwed the end of the coax onto the receptacle and then shut the compartment door. He was just about ready to leave when he heard a twig snap. That raised the hackles on the back of his neck. He looked out towards the back of the park. He could hear more movement. He crept out a little further. He turned on the flashlight, and pointed it out into the darkness. Some eyes shined back at him.

"We've got company," he said to himself, chuckling. He walked a little further out. There were several deer walking along the fence. When they saw him, they got spooked and headed away. He walked back to the coach.

"Alright, you should have cable TV now," Frank said. He walked up to the switch box that was over the passenger seat in the front, and switched to Cable input. Then he turned off the antenna booster.

"I'll run the auto program," Jane said. She got that started with the remote.

"By the way, I saw some friends out there."

"Really, who?"

"A few deer. They were over by the fence. I got pretty spooked when I heard them."

"So now you know where the fence is, eh?"

"Yes," Frank said, taking his robe off. "It's not very far back. I'm surprised we didn't see it earlier." He tossed his robe onto the bed, and then picked up his drink.

"What station do you want?" she asked.

"Either CNN or Fox. I want to see if they have anything more on the ICMBs."

"Alright. The auto program is almost done," she said. Frank walked over to the couch.

"Miss Lucy, you need to give me some space to sit down," he said. The dog looked up at him, and slowly climbed up onto Jane's lap. Frank sat down, and took another sip of his martini. He could feel the warmth of the gin flow up to his head.

"OK, here's CNN," Jane said. She selected it. The announcer was talking in front of a large map of North Korea that had flame graphics scattered around on it.

"We are getting confirmed reports that the US Air Force has been able to take out all of the missile sites in North Korea. A huge force of North Korean infantry surged across the DMZ. As soon as they reached South Korea, they surrendered. There are reports of North Korean soldiers shooting their officers at that time. The Chinese army is now pushing southward, taking out all North Korean military installations with little or no resistance."

"Shoot, I wish Red China wasn't going in there. That will just put this mess off for another day," Frank said.

"Well, I suspect there will be a flood of people going from North to South Korea in a hurry." Jane finished her martini, and leaned over against Frank. Lucy looked up at Jane's face, and then jumped off the couch and slinked off to her bed.

The news commentator was back on the screen, this time in front of a map of Europe.

"In other news, there has been widespread violence in Great Britain, France, The Netherlands, and Denmark. The Muslim minorities in those countries have come out in force to protest the actions of western countries during this crisis. Angry mobs of natives in those countries have attacked the protesters, and in almost all cases, the local police have been standing aside and letting the violence go on, resulting in injury and deaths for many of the protesters. In London the police did draw the line when a group of hooligans attempted to go into a Muslim neighborhood and pull people out of their homes."

"Wow," Frank said. "Looks like leaders of the western nations are all on the same page."

"Honey, let's go to bed now," Jane said, looking up at him.

"I don't know if I can get to sleep yet."

"Who said anything about sleep?" she replied with an embarrassed smile.

"Well, in that case," Frank said. He shut off the TV, and they walked into the bedroom.

Frank awoke to the sound of Jane puttering in the kitchen. He got up and put on his clothes, and then walked out into the salon.

"Wow, hot cakes?" Frank said, breathing in the smell of them and smiling. "What did I do to deserve that?"

Jane looked over at him and smiled.

"Take Lucy out, will you, sweetie?"

"Sure," he said. He picked up the poop bags and got Lucy hooked to her leash. She was beside herself with excitement, jumping and wagging her tail. They walked out of the door and into the warm bright sunshine. Lucy pulled Frank all around the campsite. It was a peaceful morning. Birds were chirping, and there was a soft breeze. Jane put her head up by the kitchen window.

"Hey, honey, breakfast is ready, and I've got Lucy's food in her bowl too. Is she done?"

"Yep, I'll be right in."

Frank led Lucy back to the coach. She bounded up the steps and headed right for her food dish. Mr. Wonderful was already eating. He gave Lucy an annoyed look.

The pancakes were piled up on a platter on the dinette table. Jane brought the syrup and two cups of coffee over and sat down. Frank joined her and dug in.

"Mmmmm, these are great," he said.

"Glad you like them, honey. I know it's going to be a busy day today. I thought something that will stick to your ribs was a good idea."

They were finished eating, and were enjoying their coffee when there was a knock on the door. Frank got up answered. It was Charlie and Chester.

"Good morning, folks," Charlie said. "We are going to have a meeting in the clubhouse in half an hour. Could you two make it?"

"Of course," Frank said. "We'll be there."

"Excellent, see you in a little while then," Charlie replied, and they walked over to the next space.

"Good, I figured they would want to get started pretty early," Jane said.

Frank nodded.

"I think I'll put on my good hiking shoes. I suspect I'll be walking in the underbrush and climbing up into some blinds today."

"Yes, you do that, honey," she replied as she took the empty plates to the sink. "I hope this place is defensible. I'd really like to hang out here for a while."

"Me too," Frank said as he walked back to the bedroom to retrieve his shoes. He brought them out, and then sat down on the couch and put them on.

"I guess I'd better get dressed too," Jane said. She stepped into the bedroom and dropped her robe. She was naked underneath. Frank looked over at her.

"How much time do we have?"

"Not enough, Frank," she said. Then she giggled. "Maybe later."

"We are acting like kids, aren't we?"

She looked back at him as she pulled her pants on. She had the embarrassed smile back on her face again. She was blushing.

"Yes," Jane said, pulling her t-shirt over her head as she walked back out into the salon. "But I'm glad."

"Me too," he said, putting his arm around her waist and pulling her close. "You still get me going, even after all these years." He kissed her. Her arms snaked around his neck and she held him close.

"Enough of this, or we'll miss our meeting." She giggled again.

They walked towards the door of the coach.

"Should we take Lucy with us?" Jane asked.

"You know, that isn't a bad idea," Frank said. "I'll get her leash on, and grab the bags."

The three of them left the coach and made their way to the clubhouse. They saw several other couples on their way over there as well.

"Is it OK if we bring the dog in here?" Frank asked Hilda when they got to the door.

"Sure, as long as she is on the leash and behaves," Hilda said. She squatted down and looked at Lucy. "You'll be a good girl, won't you?" Lucy nuzzled her and licked her hand.

They walked in and sat down near the front of the room. Charlie, Jeb, and Chester were up at the front of the room talking. They all nodded when they saw Frank and Jane sit down.

After about ten minutes the room was full of people. Charlie and Hilda got up in the front and motioned for everybody to sit down. A hush came over the room as people found seats.

"Thank you all so much for coming," Hilda said. She looked over at Charlie.

"Good morning, folks," Charlie said. We want to do three things today. We'd like your help with this, but it's not mandatory."

"We're with you Charlie," somebody said from the back of the room. A lot of people made affirmative comments.

"Good, and thanks," Charlie said. "We basically would like to see if this place can be defended against enemy scouting parties and scavengers. We will need to look at the perimeter fence, the topography, and the hunting blinds that are back there. We might need to do some repair on the blinds and the fence."

There was a murmur coming from the audience, and most people nodded in the affirmative.

"Secondly, we would like to know how many of you have experience with firearms. How many of you were in the military or other armed organizations?"

About one third of the men in the room raised their hands.

"Wow, that's pretty good," Charlie said. "And how many of you have firearms and ammo with you?"

Almost everybody in the room raised their hands.

"Excellent," Charlie said. "Oh, and how many of you are deer hunters, and know how to dress game?"

About ten people raised their hands.

"Good, then we know we aren't going to starve," Charlie said with a grin. "As most of you know, there is a ton of game around here."

"Can we ask a few questions?" asked one man. He was tall and thin, and looked like somebody who had been in the military. "My name is Jerry."

"Of course, Jerry. Fire away," said Charlie.

"Thank you. What's our water source? Is there a well here, or are we on city water?"

Hilda stood back up.

"We have city water, and it is still flowing," Hilda said. "The infrastructure is fairly new. Before they put that in, we were on well water. We still have the well, so if anything happens with the city, we will still have plenty of water."

"How about power?" Jerry asked.

"We are good there, too," Hilda said. "We have city power. Most of it comes from the Glen Canyon dam – Lake Powell. We also have three diesel generators. It might be a good idea to make a fuel run, though. We have some fuel, but the tanks aren't full."

"Thanks," Jerry said. "One more question….are there other RV Parks nearby that we might be able to join forces with?"

"There are several others, but the closest one is over five miles from here. Not exactly walking distance. I know the owners of all the nearby parks, though, and have good relations with all of them, so I'm sure we could help each other out in a pinch."

"Thanks," Jerry said. He sat down.

"Alright," Charlie said. "Any other questions?"

He looked around the room. Nobody else spoke up.

"How about some volunteers for checking out the back fence and the blinds?" Charlie asked.

Frank raised his hand. So did Jeb, and Jerry, and a few others.

"Excellent," Charlie said. "We could also use some people to help Hilda check out the fencing in front of the park."

Jane raised her hand, along with Chester and several other people.

"Perfect, thanks. Any other questions before we get started?"

"Any word on the battle down south?" asked Jerry.

"No, not really. We aren't seeing much on the news, and I can't get a call through to my neighbors down there. Phone lines and cell towers may have been hit."

There was another murmur through the room.

"Perhaps some of you who aren't working with the perimeter teams could start listening to the radio and watching the local TV," Hilda said. "Do any of you have shortwave?"

One person raised his hand. He was an old frail looking gentlemen.

"My name is Arthur," the man said. "I'm a ham radio operator, and I have a system in my rig. I'll get on it."

"That would be great, Arthur. Thanks," Charlie said. "Alright, we best get started. We have a long day ahead of us."

"Have fun, honey," Frank said. "You want to handle Lucy or should I? Or should I put her in the coach?"

"I'll take her," Jane said. "If she gets in the way I'll put her in the coach and turn on the air conditioner."

"May want to turn on the AC either way," Frank said. "Mr. Wonderful is in there."

"Oh, yeah."

Charlie heard what they were saying.

"Frank, there's a gate back behind the row that you're in. We'll go back that way, so you can stop off at your rig on the way."

"Sounds good, thanks."

Frank gave Jane a kiss on the forehead, and reached down and petted Lucy on the head. Then he followed Jeb and Charlie and Jerry out the door and towards the back of the park. He slipped into his coach and turned on their AC as they went by. The gate was down a curvy path, about thirty yards behind the coach. Charlie pulled a key out of his pocket and unlocked the large padlock. The gate opened with a creak. Behind it was trees and boulders and shrubs.

"Lots of cover back here," Jerry said. "It would be easy for somebody to watch us and not be seen."

"I was thinking the same thing," Frank said. "I'm Frank, by the way."

"Yes, I know who you are. I was in Williams, saw all of that stuff. I owe you, sir."

Frank smiled and nodded.

"You were military, I suspect," Frank said.

"Marine," he replied. "That was a lot of years ago, but once a marine, always a marine."

Frank nodded. Charlie stopped.

"Let's split up," Charlie said. Two of us go back to the left, and two of us to the right. Follow the fence all the way to where it joins up with the front section."

"How do we know the front section?" asked Jeb.

"The chain link turns to wrought iron," Charlie replied.

Frank and Jeb went to the left. They walked along silently, looking around them.

"Look, there's one of the deer blinds," Jeb said, pointing.

"Wow, good eyes. That's hard to see," Frank said. "Should we go check it out?"

"Let's finish with the fence first."

"OK," Frank said. There was a curve ahead of them, which they followed around.

"It looks to me like there has been somebody around here recently," Jeb said. "Look at the pine needles and the dirt over there." He pointed.

"This is getting close to the space I'm in," Frank said. "When I was out hooking up the cable TV line last night, I heard some rustling around. I pointed my flashlight over there, and saw several deer. They split in a hurry."

"Really, they went running because of a flashlight? Usually they freeze."

"Oh, crap, look at that," Frank said, stopping in his tracks and looking at the fence.

"Oh oh," Jeb said, looking down. A couple of the chain links had been cut. There was a large pair of bolt cutters laying on the ground, and a large knife… perhaps a bayonet. Jeb crouched down and started looking around.

{ 6 }

Back in the Woods

Jeb and Frank stared down at the bolt cutters and the knife. They looked at each other.

"We should be armed when we are out here," Jeb said.

"I was thinking the same thing," Frank replied.

Jeb was crouching down, giving the bolt cutters a closer look.

"Well," he said, "They haven't been here for a long time, because they don't have dirt on them. I think we're safe for the moment, though, because whoever left them here did so several hours ago. Look at the dew on them."

"What time does the dew fall?"

"Dew doesn't fall, it condenses when the air gets cold enough. I'm thinking that whoever dropped these got spooked when you shined a flashlight over here last night."

"Hmmmmm," Frank said, rubbing his chin. "That tells me that they don't belong to enemy soldiers. This is local scavengers."

"You are probably right about that. I don't think experienced soldiers would have dropped their tools when a flashlight shined at them. This might have been kids."

Frank pulled his cellphone out of his pocket and took several pictures of the fence and the tools.

"Do you have a sidearm, Frank?"

"Boy, do I," he replied, chuckling. Jeb gave him a quizzical look.

"What, do you have a derringer or something?"

"No, I've got a Ruger Blackhawk .44 mag."

"Wow. Planning on hunting some wild boar?"

"We left Redondo Beach in a hurry. I have a .44 mag Winchester lever gun, and thought bringing the old hand cannon would be a good idea, because they both use the same ammo."

"Well, good idea, as long as you can shoot the thing. After their first shot, most people flinch as they try to pull the trigger. There's a lot of blast and recoil when one of those things go off. What size barrel?"

"Big – 7 ½ inches. It's really not bad to shoot because it's heavy. I'm pretty good with it too, but it's a little much to shove into your belt."

"You got a holster?"

"Yeah, but it's an old west style.....you know, low, with a tie on the leg. Quick draw." He laughed.

"Well, I think from now on you should be wearing that thing more often than not. I'm going to do the same, but we should discuss this at the clubhouse."

"No problem. What do you have?"

"Colt .45 auto," Jeb said, "among others."

"I have one of those at home. Nice, but I can shoot the .44 mag more accurately. Would have brought it anyway, but I only had half a box of ammo."

"You have a lot of .44 mag ammo?"

"Yeah, quite a bit."

"Any other guns?"

"A 12 gauge. Good alley cleaner."

Jeb laughed.

"You sound like my granddad. He was a cop on the south side of Chicago. That's what they called their pumps."

"I'll bet he used an 1897 Winchester."

"You know your guns," Jeb said with a grin. "And yeah, that's exactly what they used."

"Let's leave this here and continue down the fence. Then we need to tie in with the others about it."

Jeb nodded, and they kept walking. There were no other problems with the fence. They got to the front section, and saw Jane and Chester coming their way. Lucy saw Frank and her tail started wagging. Jane let go of the leash and she ran over to Frank.

"Those Jack Russell's are good little watchdogs," Jeb said, bending down to let Lucy sniff his hand. "You should bring her along when we are stomping around back here. She will know somebody is coming before we do."

"That's why I wanted Jane to take her," Frank said. He picked up the leash and they continued on.

"Look, there's another blind," Jeb said, pointing. Frank nodded.

"Lucy was in a hurry to get to you," Jane said, as she walked up with Chester. "How did things look back there?"

Jeb looked at Frank, and nodded.

"We found evidence of somebody trying to cut their way in," Frank said. "There are a few links cut in the fence, and they left bolt cutters and a knife laying on the ground."

"Recent?" asked Chester. Jane looked at Frank with fear in her eyes.

"I would say last night," Jeb said. "There's no dirt on the tools, but they were covered with dew. I think Frank spooked them last night when he shined his flashlight back there."

"Either that or the deer scared them when they bolted," Frank said. "The good news is that this probably wasn't the enemy. This was probably just local scavengers. Maybe even kids. I'll bet Hilda will have some insight."

"I heard her talking about kids going back there to drink," Chester said. "She has flood lights back there. Maybe we ought to be having those on for the time being. It will probably keep the locals from trying to come in and rip us off."

"She has lights?" asked Jeb. "Yes, we definitely should be turning those on at night. How were things on the front section of the fence?"

"Everything looked good," Jane said. "The brush and trees aren't dense in the front, so I doubt any scavengers would try to get in. If it was some of the enemy army, that's another matter. They'd blow through there in no time."

"Look, here comes Charlie and Hilda and Jerry," Chester said, pointing.

Lucy barked, but she was wagging her tail.

"Well, see anything?" Charlie asked.

"Yes," Jeb said. "Somebody tried to cut their way in last night."

"How do you know that?" asked Hilda.

"There are a couple of chain links cut, and there is a set of bolt cutters and a knife sitting on the ground."

Hilda got a worried look on her face.

"How do you know it's recent?" she asked.

"They weren't covered with dirt," Jeb replied. "I suspect they are local scavengers or maybe even kids."

"I might have spooked them last night," Frank said, "when I was looking at some deer back there. I turned on my flashlight and pointed it back there. The deer got spooked and ran. Maybe that scared them."

"Does the fence need any repair?" asked Hilda.

"Not much," Jeb said. "We could wire it shut. The hole isn't big enough to crawl through. You could stick your arm through it, but you'd probably get cut."

"Alright, I've got some wire in the shed," Hilda said. "It probably was just kids. There's a stream and some shallow caves back about 200 yards. Teenagers like to drink there. We've had them sneak into the park and steal liquor before. Most people don't lock up their coaches when they walk over to the clubhouse. Some folks even leave ice chests next to their coaches at night. Easy pickings for a few beers."

"Maybe we should turn on the lights back there at night," Jeb said.

"I'll do that," Hilda said. "I usually only do that on big weekends and after the big football games and dances at the high school. They kind of ruin the rustic ambiance."

"We didn't see any problems at all on the other side of the back fence," Charlie said. "Saw one deer blind that looks like it may be usable with a little work."

"No problems with the front fencing on the other side, either," Hilda said.

"Good," Jeb said. "What next?"

"I think we should check out the blinds," Charlie said, "and fix that part of the fence. Maybe we also should go check out those caves and see if there is evidence that kids were back there last night."

"Sounds like a good plan," Hilda said. "Then we can meet in the clubhouse and figure out how we will go forward."

"One other thing," Jeb said. "I think we should be armed when we are back behind the park. Especially if we are going to go poking around back by the caves."

"I agree," Jerry said. "We probably should have worn side arms before we went back there this morning."

"We were thinking the same thing," Frank said.

"I'm fine with that, boys," Hilda said. "As long as you don't wear them inside the park."

"If we have reason to believe that the enemy is going to send scouts around here, we ought to have some people in the park carrying side arms too," Jerry said.

Hilda was silent for a moment, thinking. She had a frown on her face.

Robert Boren

"Alright, I'd be open to that, I guess," she said. "But we need to have a reasonable suspicion that we are in some danger. I don't want anybody getting drunk and accidentally shooting somebody."

"Agreed," Charlie said. "We should discuss this more with the entire group, but for now, being armed while in the woods is prudent."

"Let's go back into the park," Hilda said. "Who's going to help me fix the fence?"

"I'll do that, sweetie," Charlie said.

"Alright, then you can follow me to the shed and we'll get the wire and tools out. How about the blinds?"

Jeb, Frank, and Jerry all raised their hands.

"Great, thanks," Hilda said.

"I'd love to help, but I can't climb trees anymore," said Chester.

Hilda smirked at him.

"Not to worry, Chester. Why don't you go talk to Arthur and see if he found anything out on his short wave radio?"

"Will do," he said.

They walked through the front gate of the park. Charlie and Hilda walked over to the shed together.

"I'll meet you guys at the back gate," Frank said. "I'm going to go get my pistol."

"Sounds like a plan," Jeb said. "Half an hour?"

"Sounds good to me," Frank said.

"Agreed," said Jerry. They all took off towards their rigs.

"Are you buying the kid story about the hole in the fence?" asked Jane as she walked with Frank and Lucy.

"It sounds plausible, but I'll reserve judgment. I don't think it was an enemy scouting party. I don't think a flashlight would have scared those folks off. I'd probably be dead right now if they were back there." After he said that, Frank wished he hadn't. Jane looked up at him, her brow furrowed. She looked scared.

"I'm going back there with you," Jane said. "With Lucy and the shotgun. I'll keep watch while you are up in the tree."

"Are you sure that's a good idea?"

"Yes, I am," Jane said. "And I won't take no for an answer."

Frank nodded.

They got back to the coach, unlocked it, and went in. The AC had been on for a while, and it was nice inside.

"Let's have a snack," Jane said. 'I'm going to wear that small backpack and put some water in it."

"Smart idea," Frank said. "I'm going bring the other backpack. I'll put the hatchet in there, and a hammer, and some nails, and that folding saw. I've got all that stuff in my tool box. You might want to throw a paper bowl in your backpack for Lucy, and some treats. We may be out there for a few hours."

Frank went outside to the back compartment, and grabbed the tools and a box of large nails. He set them on the table under the awning, and then went back into the coach to get his pistol. Jane was loading up her backpack when he got in there.

"Find what you needed?" she asked.

"Yep. I'll bring out the shotgun. You might want to toss a box of shells into your backpack."

She nodded. Frank went into the bedroom, and opened the rear closet. He pulled the belt and holster out, and then pulled out a box of ammo. He quickly loaded the belt loops with .44 mag cartridges, and then put on the belt. Then he reached back into closet and pulled out his pistol. He checked it.....only one bullet missing. The one that he shot Officer Simmons with. He pulled a cartridge out of the box and put it into the cylinder, and then put the pistol into the holster. He tied the bottom leather lace around his leg. Then he picked up the shotgun and a box of shells on the way out of the bedroom.

"Here you go, honey," Frank said, leaning the shotgun against the dinette bench. "It's loaded, and the safety is on. Be careful."

"Wow, nice old west look there, partner," Jane said. She snickered.

Frank shrugged his shoulders, and picked up his backpack. He took it outside and loaded his tools, then carried it back into the coach.

"Want a Clif Bar?" he asked.

"Sure, why not," Jane said.

Frank took two bars out of the pantry, and they devoured them while standing next to the kitchen counter. They washed them down with water from the fridge dispenser.

"I'm ready, sweetie," Frank said. He slipped the backpack over his shoulders, and walked out the door, waiting for Jane. She put her backpack on, grabbed Lucy's leash, and herded her outside. Frank closed the door and locked it.

When they got to the back gate Jeb was already there.

"Hi, folks," said Jeb. "Brought the dog and a shotgun. Good idea."

"Hi, Jeb," Frank said. Jane looked over at Jeb, nodded, and smiled. She felt really self-conscious holding the shotgun.

"Here comes Jerry," Jeb said, looking past the couple. Frank and Jane turned around and saw him. He was walking up with a rifle. It was hanging off one of his shoulders on a sling.

"No sidearm, huh?" asked Jeb.

"I've got one, but I'm a better shot with this and don't mind carrying it," he said. "Is there a showdown at high noon, Hoss?" He was looking at Frank's western style belt and holster. He chuckled.

Frank shrugged, with a sheepish grin on his face.

"Guess it's going to take me a while to live this down," he said. "What's that you have?"

"Oh, this is just an old M-1 Carbine. Handy but not very powerful. The best thing about it is that it will fire as fast as I can pull the trigger."

"Oh yeah, I remember those," Frank said. "My cousin had one. Uses that .30 Carbine round. No recoil at all, and a lot of fun to shoot."

"Yes, it's fun to shoot, but if you have to stop somebody, better hit them in the right place," Jerry said dryly. "Let's go. Charlie left the gate unlocked for us. He's already over at the hole in the fence with Hilda."

Jeb opened the gate and walked out, followed by the rest of the team. The woods really captured Lucy's interest. She was trying to pull ahead of Frank.

"Settle down, girl, we will be out here for a while," Frank said.

"You want to split up?" asked Frank.

"Yeah, you can go with Jeb and I'll take care of Jane," Jerry said. Then he laughed. Jane didn't look very amused.

"No, I think I'll take Jane with me, thanks," said Frank, taking it as a joke.

"Of course, just joking around," he said. "My wife might be a little upset if I did that. She's the jealous type."

"Is she here?" Jane asked. "Your wife, I mean."

"Yes, she's in the coach with my mother-in-law."

Jeb cracked up.

"Doesn't sound like much of a vacation."

"Actually I like my wife's mom Rosie a hell of a lot," Jerry said. "That old broad can drink me under the table, too." He laughed again. Jane gave him a sideways glance.

"Jane and I will take that one," Frank said, pointing of to the blind on the right.

"Sounds good," Jeb said. "We'll take the one that's a little past that, towards the front section of fence."

They split up.

"Wow, get a load of that guy," Jane said. "Did you think that was funny?"

"No. Wonder what his wife is like?"

"Good question. I imagine we'll find out sooner or later."

"I don't think she was at the clubhouse meeting. I remember Jerry, but he was there alone. He asked a lot of questions."

"He seemed serious at that meeting. Not so much today. Maybe he's just coming off of the stress."

"Possible," Frank said. The stopped in front of the trees where the blind was.

"Wow, that's pretty tall," Jane said.

"Yes, it looks taller up close than I expected. I'm going to have to go up slowly and hammer a nail or two into each of those rail pieces to make sure it stays fastened to the trees."

"I don't like this. Be careful," Jane said. Frank took off his backpack and put in on the ground. Lucy ran up and sniffed it.

"Sorry girl, the treats are in mom's backpack."

He pulled out the hammer and the box of nails. Then he turned and looked at the tree.

The blind was looked nice. It was set into three trees that were close together. The ladder was home made. There were two by fours for the edges; two ten foot pieces on each side, bolted together. The rungs looked very strong. They were held to the two by fours with carriage bolts and nuts. Frank grabbed it and shook it. It was solid, from what he could tell.

"It actually feels pretty good. I'm going climb it slowly, with some nails in my shirt pocket and the hammer in my belt."

"Alright. I'll be watching."

"If Lucy starts to growl, make sure I know about it."

Jane nodded. She had a worried look on her face.

Frank started up. The ladder was sturdy. The rails were nailed into the tree every so often, but that wasn't the main thing holding it. Frank could see that the tops of the rail were bolted onto the bottom frame of the blind above.

"Nice job on this," he said to himself. He started climbing up faster, feeling more confident. There was one spot where the rails were coming loose slightly, about two thirds of the way up. He got the hammer out, and pulled a couple of nails out of his pocket. He hammed a nail into each of the rails and on into the tree. That made it feel a little sturdier. He got to the top and looked at the wall, which was on a hinge, with a handle on the bottom. He pulled the door open far enough to get in. The inside was much nicer than he expected. It was triangular, bolted into the trees in such a way that the trees could move in the wind but the blind could float with it. There was a bench that ran along the back two walls of the triangle. There was a safety rail that could be lowered across the front when the blind was occupied. It had a hinge on it, and was in the up position. The door could be fastened to that so you wouldn't fall out. Frank hoisted himself up and stood on the platform. The walls were about chest high. He tried sections of the floor with his feet. It was solid. Not even any termite damage. It was all pressure treated lumber. Frank wondered how the builder hoisted all of this heavy wood up here.

"Wow, this thing is great," Frank shouted down to Jane.

"Good. Be careful."

Frank laughed to himself. There was a large wooden chest in the middle of the floor, about three feet high. It looked like it was used as a table. Somebody used marine varnish on the top, to seal it up. He sat down on the bench and looked around. Sitting down, you could just see over the walls. Perfect. He noticed that the top of the table had a hinge. He pulled it up. It creaked, but opened easily.

Frank started to laugh as he looked inside.

"What's so funny?" shouted Jane.

"You have to see this," he shouted down to her.

7

Up in the Blinds

Jane looked up at the blind. Frank was still up there laughing.

"Honey, you really need to come up here and check this out."

"I'm afraid to climb up there," she said.

"It's really easy. The ladder is sturdy. You can make it."

"What about Lucy?"

"Tie her to that small tree over there. And leave your backpack down there if you'd feel better."

"Alright, but if I get scared part way up, I'm going back down."

"No problem."

Jane led Lucy over to the small tree. She tied her up there, but took her backpack with her.

"What about the shotgun?" she shouted.

"Just a minute….I'll come down far enough to grab it from you."

Frank got back on the ladder and quickly climbed down. Jane held up the shotgun and Frank grabbed it by the receiver. He turned and climbed back up with it. Jane started up. Lucy was watching her, and barked a couple of times.

"Quiet down, girl," Jane said. "I'll be back down in a few minutes."

Robert Boren

Jane made her way up. It was much easier than she thought it would be. Frank held the wall open for her and she climbed up. When she was inside Frank pulled the wall shut and put down the safety rail.

"Wow, this is pretty nice," Jane said, looking around. "It's like a kid's clubhouse."

"Sure is. Look at the view, too. You can see quite a ways. See the stream over there?" He pointed.

"Yes. Very charming up here. So what was so funny?"

"Sit down," Frank said. He motioned to a spot on the bench. She sat, and Frank sat next to her. Then he raised the table top back on its hinge until it was all the way open.

"Good Lord," she said, laughing. "I wonder if Hilda knows about this."

Frank laughed. "I doubt it."

The chest contained several bottles of whiskey, a bottle of gin, and some shot glasses. There was a small kerosene heater in there with a can of fuel, some playing cards, and a stack of girly magazines.

"This was a man cave.....err man treehouse," Jane said, laughing. The items in the chest were a little dusty, but it didn't look like they ever got wet.

"Yeah, I'll bet Hilda's late husband spent a fair amount of time up here. All the comforts of home."

"No bathroom, though," Jane said.

"Well, most of the time a man wouldn't have a problem."

"Eeewwww!" Jane said. "Hope it didn't land all over the ladder."

Frank cracked up.

"Should we tell Hilda about this?" he asked.

"I don't think we should. I'd mention it to Charlie, and he can tell her if he thinks she would want to know."

"Sounds reasonable," Frank said. "Maybe we could sneak up here for a little fun from time to time." He grinned.

"No chance, buster," she said. "Somebody would hear us."

"Oh, alright," he said, trying to give her a pouty look. She laughed, and put her hand on his shoulder.

"You want to go back down?" Frank asked.

"In a minute. I want to look out in all directions," she said. She stood up and did a slow turn around. "You can hardly see the park from here. Too many trees."

"Yes, but you can see the stream and surrounding areas back there really well. I'll bet this was a prime hunting spot because of that."

"It's probably going to be a good sentry post too," Jane said. "If kids are drinking down by the caves and the stream, there must be an easy way there. I didn't see anything in the front half of the park that looked like a good route to get back there."

"We'll have to check that out," Frank said.

"It's really beautiful up here," Jane said.

"Yes it is. I could spend some time up here."

"With the booze and magazines?"

They both cracked up.

"Alright," Jane said. "I'm ready to get down now."

"OK, I'll hold the door open for you." He flipped up the safety bar and pushed the wall out of the way. Jane carefully got back on the ladder and started down. Frank closed the top of the chest, and then followed her down. Lucy started barking when she saw them coming, her tail wagging.

"Where to now?" Jane asked, as she untied Lucy from the tree.

"You want to go check out the caves?"

"Sure, now that we know where they are."

"Alright," Frank said. "You want the shotgun back?"

"Sure," she said. Frank handed it to her, and they walked towards the creek. They could hear the rushing water as they approached.

"Wow, look at this," Frank said, pointing to a small waterfall that flowed into a large pool.

"Yes, I can see why kids want to hang around here," Jane said. They walked over to the water's edge and looked. There was some evidence of people being here – little pieces of litter here and there, but it wasn't terrible.

"That must be the caves," Frank said, pointing to a stone wall about 30 yards to their left. They made their way up there, over a well beaten path.

"I don't think I'd call these caves," Jane said. "More like a series of rock outcroppings. They aren't very deep."

"Just enough to get out of the sun or the rain," Frank said. He climbed back into the first one. The floor was stone. You could almost stand in there.

"Look over to your right, Frank. Beer cans."

Frank went over there and picked one up. He shook it back and forth and listened, then smelled the opening.

"Yep, it was probably kids last night alright. There is still some beer residue in the can. It smells fresh."

"I'll bet the kids were on a hunt for more to drink, like Hilda suspected. I'll be in there in a minute to take a few pictures with my iPHONE."

Frank nodded. Then he laughed.

"What?" Jane asked as she got under the outcropping.

"Condom wrappers," Frank said, pointing.

"Well, I guess this is better than the back seat of a car," Jane said. She giggled. "As long as they brought a blanket or something."

"Another place we could try out, perhaps?"

"I'm not a teenager anymore, Frank," she said, looking at him and smirking. Frank laughed.

Lucy growled, and then barked a couple of times, looking towards the stream. Frank put his hand on his pistol, and Jane froze.

"Frank, that you back there?"

It was Jeb.

"Yeah, Jeb, we're up here," he replied. "We found evidence that kids were here, probably last night."

Lucy growled again as Jeb walked up, but then she stopped when she realized that she knew him.

"I told you it was a good idea to have your dog with you," Jeb said, smiling. "What did you find?"

"These beer cans," Frank said, pointing over to them. "They are still wet inside, and they smell fresh."

"Figures," Jeb said. "Is that what you guys were laughing about?"

Jane looked at Jeb, her face turning read. Then she looked up at Frank.

"You can tell him about that," she said. Jeb looked over at Frank.

"Oh, it's nothing, just some condom wrappers," Frank said.

Jeb looked embarrassed.

"Sorry, Jane," he said.

"For what? I was just a little embarrassed."

"Where's Jerry?" Frank asked.

"His wife called him and asked that he come back after we were done with the blind. He went back to his rig."

"How was the blind?"

"Pretty beat up, but we hammered it back together. How about the one you guys were at?"

"It's perfect," Frank said. "Very sturdy. I had to drive a couple of nails in on the ladder, but other than that it's in real good shape." Jane started to giggle.

"What?" Jeb asked.

"It looks like that blind was a man cave for Hilda's departed husband," she said.

Jeb started to crack up. "Oh, really? Do tell."

"There's a chest in the middle of the floor….there's several bottles of whiskey and some girly magazines in there."

Jeb laughed out loud.

"That sounds like old Jer. I really miss that old coot."

"Do you think Hilda knows about it?"

"The girly magazines? Probably not. Maybe the booze. I'd have to ask Charlie."

"Yeah, we were going to ask him about this before we say anything to Hilda," Frank said.

"Probably a good idea," Jeb said. "Charlie knew those two better than anybody."

"Why don't we get back," Jane said. "I think we're done here."

"Alright, but I do want to do one more thing first. Let's see where the kids are coming in from." Frank said.

"Oh, yeah, forgot about that," Jane said. They walked out of the outcropping and down to the stream. You could see a path beaten down along the water. The stream got smaller as they made their way up from the water fall.

"It's so pretty here," Jane said.

The path ended at a thin spot in the creek that had several flat topped rocks in the water, and you could see the trail picking up on the other side. They walked over the rocks to the far bank. About twenty yards from the creek was a large clearing. There were tire tracks on it.

"Well, this is where they park," Jeb said.

"Looks like it," Frank said.

They continued on towards the dirt road that led from the clearing. It was as pretty as the creek was, with trees lining both sides. There was a two lane blacktop about fifty yards out.

"There's the road. Wonder which one it is?" Frank asked.

Jane pulled out her iPHONE and brought up the map application. It found GPS right away.

"Red Rock road," Jane said. "I'll bet Hilda knows where this goes."

"Probably," Jeb said. "I vaguely remember that road, but I didn't know about this clearing. I think the road runs between the little town and some ranches."

"Well, at least we know about one of the back ways in now," Frank said. "Let's go back and talk to the others."

Jane and Jeb nodded, and they started back. It was a little warmer now, and the shade of the trees was a nice break in between the stretches of hot sunshine. Birds were chirping, and a gentle breeze was just starting to come up.

"What time is it, anyway," asked Jeb.

"Almost 1:00," Jane said after looking at her phone.

They could see the back fence now. Charlie came walking out to the gate to meet them.

"Hi, folks, how'd it go?"

"We checked out the caves and the stream, and found where the kids are getting in, off of Red Rock road," Frank said.

"Yeah, and we found fresh beer cans in one of the caves. Looks like they were there last night alright," Jane said.

"Well, I think that's good news," Charlie said. "We got the fence buttoned back up."

"Good," Frank said.

"How about the blinds?"

"Jerry and I fixed the one closest to the front of the park," Jeb said.

"Where is Jerry?" asked Charlie.

"His wife called him and asked him to come back to the rig as soon as we were done, so he hi-tailed it. I went over to the stream and ran into these two."

"And how about the other blind?" Charlie asked.

"It's in tip top shape," Frank said. "I had to drive a couple of nails in to keep the ladder from wobbling, but it's bolted at the top, so it wasn't really dangerous before I did that."

"How well did you know Hilda's husband?" asked Jane.

"Jer? He was a good friend. A really funny guy. I miss him a lot," Charlie said. "Why?"

"He had this blind set up like a little man cave, complete with whiskey and girly magazines."

Charlie laughed.

"Yep, that's Jer," he said. "He did have a little bit of a drinking problem. Hilda used to get mad at him for getting drunk and getting too sentimental. She made him get all of his booze out of the house."

"Well, that explains it. Does Hilda know about this stuff, or should we keep our mouths shut?" asked Jane.

"Well, she may not know about this particular stash, but I'm sure she wouldn't be surprised," Charlie said. "Why don't you let me break it to her?"

"Alright, sounds good," Jane said.

"That blind could be pretty useful," Frank said. "A person could spend a lot of time up there on watch with no problem, and they would have a commanding view of the area in back of the property. You really can't see the RV Park from the blind, though."

"Probably why Jer picked that one for his man cave," Jeb said, laughing.

"There's also a kerosene heater up there, and some fuel," Frank said.

"Well, depending on what Chester finds out, we might want to station somebody back there. I hope not, though," Charlie said. "Might as well get back. I'll lock this gate back up for now." He closed and locked the gate, and then the four of them started walking in towards the clubhouse.

"I think we should drop off the guns and the dog," Frank said. "Jane and I will be at the clubhouse in a few minutes."

"Alright," Charlie said.

"I'd better go dump off my pistol too," Jeb said. He headed off to his rig.

Frank and Jane got to their door in a couple of minutes, and Frank unlocked it. Cool air rolled out.

"Ah, it will be nice in here," Jane said as she followed Lucy up the steps. Frank followed, and shut the door behind him.

"Well, what do you think? Can we keep good enough track of this place to be safe here for a while?" asked Jane.

"From scavengers and kids, yes," Frank said. "From the enemy, not a chance. We need to find out what is going on down south. Hopefully the guy with the ham radio can give us some info."

"Hopefully," Jane said. "Wonder if Jerry's wife is going to show up?"

"Good question," Frank said. "And I wonder how Hilda is going to take the news of what was in that blind."

"I'm really glad that Charlie offered to bring that up."

"Ready to go?" Frank asked.

"Sure, let's go."

They left their coach and headed for the clubhouse.

"Remind me to call Sarah later. I want to find out if she's still coming or not," Jane said as they were walking.

"I was wondering about that too. I hope they called off the evacuation before she got too far. Portland is probably safer than being on the road."

"Exactly what I was thinking," Jane said. They got to the door of the clubhouse. Charlie saw them from the far side of the room, and motioned for them to come over. He was leaning against the cabinet in the front, next to Hilda and Chester.

"So, you found Jer's stash, eh," Hilda said. She cracked up. "I told him he could only drink up there. That way, he'd have to sober up before he could come down. He was kind of a sloppy drunk, bless his heart. I got tired of being around it."

"Do you want me to do anything with that stuff? Bring it down here?" asked Frank.

"Girly magazines, no," she said with a smirk. "I don't know about the rest. I suppose you could bring the booze down here, but I don't really see any reason to. I've got plenty here in the clubhouse."

"Maybe we should leave it if we have to post somebody up there," Chester said.

"As long as it's somebody who isn't going to drink a bunch of it and pass out on the job," Charlie said. They all cracked up.

"You could bring those girly magazines down to me," Chester said with a grin.

They all started laughing. Chester's face turned red.

"Hey, Chester, did you get any info from the ham radio guy?" asked Frank.

"Arthur," Chester said. "He hasn't been able to raise anybody down there yet. He did talk to somebody in Tucson. We kicked their butts down there, but it was a bloody mess."

"Well, maybe they can move the troops from Tucson up to Phoenix," Charlie said.

"I think that's what they were telling Arthur they were going to do."

"Hey, look, here comes Jerry," Jeb said. "Looks like he has his women with him this time."

Frank and Jane looked around. Jerry was walking slowly with an old Asian woman, who had a big smile on her face. Jerry was holding her upper arm to keep her steady. On her other arm was a younger attractive Asian woman. She looked to be about ten years younger than Jerry.

Jane got close to Frank and whispered.

"Mail order?"

Frank just laughed.

They approached slowly. Jerry had a big grin on his face.

"Hi, folks," he said. "This is Rosie and Jasmine. Girls, this is Charlie, Chester, Hilda, Jeb, Frank, and Jane."

Jasmine got a shy smile on her face and said hello. Rosie was more outgoing. She beamed.

"Hi, so nice to meet you all," She said, in heavy Philippine accent. "When happy hour?"

Everybody cracked up.

"Oh, I think we can rustle up some drinks after the meeting," Hilda said, grinning. "Why don't we get the business part of this over with? Looks like most everybody is here."

Charlie stood up in front.

"Can I have everybody's attention, please?"

A hush settled over the room. People found seats.

"We finished a survey of the fence, the cave area, and the woods behind the property. We think it is fairly secure, but we do have an incident to bring up."

There was murmuring amongst the crowd.

"We had somebody attempt to cut through the chain link fencing in the back of the park last night. We think they got spooked when Frank shined a flashlight back there."

More murmuring.

"Are we safe here?" asked a woman near the front.

"We believe that we are, at least for now," Hilda said. "We have evidence that the attempt was made by some local kids. Fresh beer cans were found down in the caves by the stream. This isn't new. Teenagers like to drink back there. Every once in a while they will try to get into the park looking for ice chests that have beer in them."

"What are we going to do about it," asked another person.

"I have flood lights installed in the back. I will start turning them on at night. That should keep the kids away," she said. "I use them for nights when I know there is going to be activity back there, like after high school football games and dances."

Charlie took the floor again.

"We've checked out the deer blinds that are in the trees back there, and made some repairs. If it appears that we are going to have trouble, we could post sentries out in those. They have a good view of the area. We will be able to see people coming into the area behind the park from those blinds."

"How do we know if we will need to?" asked the woman up front.

"Well, hopefully we will get some news from Arthur about what is going on in Arizona. We have gotten some good news. The US Army has defeated the enemy in Tucson. There have been reports that troops are now being moved up to the Phoenix area to take care of the rest of the enemy there, and act as a staging point to clean up the Islamist army coming from west Texas."

"Yep," Chester said. "There are reports on both the cable news outlets and local news stations that a battle is raging in Phoenix right now, and the enemy is running low on supplies."

"And therein lies our main concern," Charlie said. "We might have raiding parties coming north into Utah looking for supplies and ammo. We believe those are the only people we would need to worry about."

"What about Flagstaff?" asked somebody in the back of the room.

"The city has been locked down, but apparently no attack has come yet," Chester said. "There is still some fighting going on to the south and east of Flagstaff, but it's slowing down. We think they aren't getting supplies anymore. The Texans have sealed up their southern border, and the US Army has sealed up the southern Arizona border."

"We can see all of that stuff on the TV channels right now," Jerry said. "That's not the info we need, though. We need to know if there are enemy forces moving past Flagstaff to the northwest, where we just came from."

"Nobody knows that more than I do," Charlie said. "I have an RV Park there that I'm concerned about. The problem is that there isn't any big population centers there, so the news outlets aren't focusing on it right now. They are focusing on Tucson, Phoenix, and Flagstaff.

That's why we need Arthur to continue trying to find somebody down in that area on his ham radio."

"I take it the phone coverage down there is still messed up," Frank asked.

"Yes, I still can't get through to any of my friends down there, and it worries me, Frank," Charlie said.

"Look, here comes Arthur," said Chester, pointing to the door.

8

Security

A hush came over the clubhouse as Arthur slowly walked in. He approached Chester in the front of the room.

"Arthur, do you have any news?" Chester asked.

"Yeah, are the Islamists getting close to Tusayan?" asked Jeb.

"Islamists, no," Arthur said. "They are just about done. Where the army hasn't killed them off, the local people are doing the job. Convert or die doesn't work so well with the rednecks that live outside of Phoenix and Flagstaff." He laughed.

"So why aren't we seeing that on the news broadcasts?" asked Jerry.

"They are covering the Army operations pretty well," he replied. "From what I'm hearing the military battles in Phoenix and outside of Flagstaff are being covered accurately. The Geneva Convention is being followed, prisoners are taken when possible. Not so much with the citizens. They are pissed."

"Really," Charlie said. "What's happening?"

"Some of the militias are executing people they capture. Burning down mosques. Killing Islamist protesters. In some cases they are even going after moderate Muslims. Not all of these rednecks are bad, but there is an element that wants to completely destroy all vestiges of

Islam in this country. They also want their states to secede from the Union."

"I think we know something about those folks," Frank said. "Little wannabe warlords."

"Ah yes, and that brings me to Tusayan," Arthur said. "There is a militia there. It's small, but it's a bad one. They have been forcing local populations to either join them or pay tribute."

"Tribute?" asked Charlie.

"Supplies, weapons, vehicles, and so on," Arthur said. "They also demand to stay at people's homes, and have been demanding sexual favors from the women."

"So where are they?" asked Frank. "How far is their reach?"

"They are hanging out mainly between Williams and the Grand Canyon. They aren't very mobile."

"Should we be worried about these guys?" asked Jane.

"Possibly, if the Army doesn't do something about them. Right now they aren't growing, but they haven't gone away, and they may start growing eventually. I doubt they come up here, but if they do, it will probably be to find some people they are hunting."

"Oh oh," Frank said.

"Yeah, oh oh," said Chester. "I'm afraid I know who these folks are."

"They keep talking about finding the people who killed the 'Martyrs of Williams', whoever that is," Arthur said.

Frank's blood ran cold. Jane looked at him and could see it.

"They are probably looking for us," Jane said. "We killed those militia folks from Williams on our way to Tusayan."

"I had a feeling that was the case, given how many people here were in the Williams area when the shit hit the fan," Arthur said. "Chester wouldn't come clean."

Chester looked at him and shrugged his shoulders.

"You weren't in Williams?" asked Jane.

"No, I was in Tusayan when you guys arrived at Charlie's place," Arthur said.

"Is this militia facing any resistance down there?" Frank asked.

"Well, most of the more capable people from the area who would resist are here with us, apparently," Arthur said. "They do have a fly in the ointment, though."

"What would that be?" asked Charlie.

"A shadowy person called Officer Simmons."

"Oh, crap," Frank said.

"I wouldn't worry too much about him," Arthur said. "He appears to be on our side at the moment."

"I shot him when we left Williams," Frank said. "It was back when we believed what the 'Martyrs of Williams' were trying to sell us."

"I still wouldn't worry too much about him. In fact, I don't think we should worry too much about the militia either. They talk a big game, but they are a long way from here, and things aren't going that well for them. They don't have the resources to travel up here with any kind of strength. And as I said, most of the good people from there are in this campground right now. I doubt they could take us on and win. Hell, sounds like you killed the best of them. They just prey on the weak now."

"Do you know anything more about Officer Simmons?" asked Chester.

"No, not really. He works like a thief in the night. He sneaks in, kills a few people in that militia, destroys some supplies, and then disappears. He doesn't appear to be bothering anybody else."

"You know that guy was supporting the Islamist Army, don't you?" Frank asked.

"From what I've heard, this guy has been hard to read since the trouble started," Arthur said. "For all we know, he might have been helping the Feds when you ran into him."

"Then why would he try to hold us up in Williams when the Islamists were coming?"

"Several of the leaders of the Williams Militia were there," Arthur said. "Why not let one enemy take out the other? He had no way to tell if you personally were part of the militia or not."

Frank felt dizzy. His brain was spinning. He snapped himself out of it, and looked out into the crowd.

"How many of you were originally in that militia?" he asked. "Don't worry about admitting it. You are with us now. I just would like to know. Maybe you can be of some help."

About ten people raised their hands nervously.

"I'm Jackson," said one man who had his hand up. "A lot of us were in that group until we found out what they were about. We went to that campground outside Williams to get away from them, because they had the town under their control, for the most part. Then those creeps Dave, Ken, and Lewis showed up. It was right after the chief got there. It was almost like they were trying to keep an eye on him. They were asking everybody out there where he was."

The other people with their hands up nodded in agreement.

"This wasn't what we considered a militia when we joined up," said another man. "It was originally a hunting club that the chief started, but then Dave and Lewis got in and started teaching us survivalist skills. We thought it was fun at the time. You know – 'Doomsday Preppers' was on TV. These guys were like that. The person that we really thought highly of was the police chief, though, and I don't think he liked those guys. I'm wondering now if he really killed himself."

"What's your name?" Frank asked.

"Earl," he said. "I'm glad to be with you guys. I hope you don't hold any distrust. I'm not like those guys. I chose to come with you."

"I know," Frank said. "You'll get no problem from me."

Hilda stood up.

"I think we should talk about security, just in case," she said.

"Before we get into that, can Arthur fill us in about what has been happening outside of the country?" asked Jerry. "We haven't been getting very good news."

Arthur stood back up.

"I'll tell you what I know, but it's unofficial," he said. He paused until the room got quiet, and then went on. "North Korea is *gone*. The US did most of it, but Russia and China helped. A couple small devices were detonated in South Korea. We lost a lot of people, including some of our soldiers."

"Oh no," said the woman who had a son stationed there.

"Most of the Americans stationed there survived," Arthur said to her. "I'll take you back to my rig after the meeting and we'll see if we can contact the army about him."

"Thank you," she said.

"Russia was hit with small nuclear detonations in several more of her cities, basically in the same way we were. They have been wiping out radical Muslims and those associated with them within their borders, and doing the same to former USSR provinces that are just outside. The UN is complaining, but nobody cares about them at this point. They are a joke – they are at least partly responsible for this mess. Some of the worst of the enemy countries have been controlling the Human Rights commission for years, and people are finally wise. The peaceniks in the US that usually jump up and down about this sort of thing have been staying home."

"There's a shock," Frank said sarcastically.

"Yeah," Arthur said. "There haven't been any more detonations in the US. There have been a few in Europe. There was one in Italy, one in Finland, and one in Spain. Nothing as bad as what happened in Paris, though. Things have been very rough for the Muslim populations in Europe. Same with Canada and Australia. You mess with the bull long enough, and you get the horns."

"What about the Middle East?" asked Charlie.

"I was getting to that. The major cities of Iran, Syria, Iraq, Afghanistan, Libya, Saudi Arabia, Sudan, and the smaller countries along the Persian Gulf are history. Bombed flat, some with nukes, some with conventional. Pakistan was hit hard with nukes, by the US, Russia, the EU, and India. Turkey was also hit, and was kicked out of NATO."

"Turkey," Frank said. "I knew it."

"Are things settled down now?" asked Charlie.

"Yes, they are getting there," Arthur said. "Governments have turned to humanitarian work in their own countries, and in others if they have the capability."

"Anything happen to Israel?" asked Jerry.

"Somebody tried to sneak a nuke device in through a tunnel in Gaza," Arthur said. "They screwed up and detonated it there. Idiots. After that, Israel, Egypt, Jordon, and Lebanon made an alliance. They have been protecting each other, and have been able to ride out the storm with very little damage. All of those countries are now involved in humanitarian work in the region. That's about all I know, folks. You may see different things on the news for a while. It's been all over the place, but things will sort their way out."

"Thank you, Arthur," Hilda said. "Now, back to security." She glanced over at Charlie, and he stood up.

"We told you about those deer blinds," he said. "I think we should set up a schedule and ask for volunteers to man them."

"Yes," Jerry said. "And we should work out the rules for firearms. For sure anybody outside of the park should take a gun with them. We might even want to consider having some people wear side arms inside the park."

"I have reservations about carrying firearms inside the park," Hilda said. "But if we take a vote on it, I'll go with the majority."

"What about the surrounding area?" asked Jerry. "Any militia types around here? Who's in the nearby towns?"

"I'm still in contact with most of the local folks," Hilda said. "The nearest town is pretty small. About half of the people there are retired folks. The rest families. Mormons for the most part, of course, so they tend to have a lot of kids. There is good school system, with a High School.....class size usually about 80, so it's small. The economy is almost all tourism, although there are a few small ranches and farms here and there. I haven't heard anything about any militia activity around here. I doubt that the townspeople would put up with it, and since this is a rural area, they are all well-armed. There are also some rednecks living on the outskirts of town, but they aren't the militia type. They only care about hunting and their moonshine."

"How far away is the town?" asked Frank. "And do they have much in the way of supplies?"

"They are about twelve miles away," she said. "There is one other RV park between here and there, and they have a pretty good sized store. Howard, the owner, is a dear friend. That park is about five miles away. Howard has already told me that he's got a lot of stuff for sale there if we need it, because he stocked up for the tourist season, and we all know what happened to that this year. The town has a Walmart, a smaller grocery store, and several motels and restaurants. I don't know how well stocked the Walmart is at this point. Probably depends on if they were getting their trucks from the north or the south."

"How about supplies at this park?" asked Jane. "I see you have a little store up front."

"Yes, I'm pretty well stocked too. Over stocked, in fact. I would normally have more than two hundred RVs here during this season, and I stocked up on a lot of merchandise before I knew things were going crazy. So we have plenty of canned and dry goods, food and otherwise. We are running low on produce. There's very little left at this point, and I'm not sure how to get more."

"Yeah, the price has probably gone through the roof too, I would think," Jane said.

"Of course," Hilda said.

"Well, this isn't the apocalypse," Jeb said, "at least from what Arthur was saying. Things will slowly get back to normal, and most of us will be able to go back home. It might take a couple of months. It really depends on what happens down south, and if the nuclear threat is really over."

"I partially agree," Jerry said. "The US will be secured in a couple of months, but I think we are looking at over a year of action south of the border. Mexico is a mess, and what happens down there will impact what happens up here to a certain degree."

"Yes, that is something important to keep in mind," Arthur said. "There are probably still hundreds of Islamic fighters down there.....maybe thousands. The governments of the US and Mexico are going to have to root them out. They had a big pipeline of war supplies which we stopped at our borders. I'll bet there are a lot of heavy weapons that were queued up down there.....might even be more nukes."

There was a collective groan from the crowd.

"Alright, that is true enough, folks, but we should focus on the near term," Charlie said. "There's nothing we can do about the longer term problems. I say we take a few votes."

"I agree," Frank said.

"Me too," said Hilda.

People in the crowd were nodding and some were saying yes.

"How many of you would be willing and able to take turns manning the blinds in the back of the park?" asked Charlie. "You need to be young enough and strong enough to climb a tall ladder safely."

About one half of the crowd raised their hands.

"Excellent, thanks," Charlie said. "We'll put a signup sheet on the front table, and then we'll put together a schedule and place that on the wall outside the door of the clubhouse.

"The roof on the store in the front part of the park is flat with a façade around it," Hilda said. "We'll get that set up as an observation post too, and add that to the schedule. There are stairs to get up there in the back section of the store. It's easier to get up than a ladder, so if older people want to help, that might be a good alternative for them."

"Great idea," said Charlie. "Now, about firearms. We've already suggested that people who are outside the park be armed. Let's have a show of hands on carrying guns inside the park. How many are in favor?"

There was a murmur in the crowd. About a third of the people raised their hands.

"How many opposed?"

Most of the other folks raised their hands. It was a clear majority.

"OK, folks, looks like we have a clear majority against wearing guns inside the park, so we will discourage that, except for when people are walking to the outside of the park from their rigs. Anything else we should talk about today?"

"How about payment for the park spaces?" asked Jerry.

"I'll be charging the normal rates, which you can pay via credit card if you'd like," Hilda said. "The financial systems seem to still be working. If any of you has problems coming up with the rent, I'll discuss it with you on an individual basis, and we'll work something out."

"Anything else?" asked Charlie.

"I'd like to make a comment," Frank said.

"You have the floor, Frank," Charlie said.

"I'd just like to make sure all of us understand that our government, our Constitution, and our Bill of Rights are still in force. We can make decisions on how to weather the rough times and protect ourselves, but bottom line is that our societal norms, our laws, and our constitutional protections remain in force. Does anybody disagree with that?"

There was a smattering of no comments, and most people shook their heads no. Jane looked up at Frank and smiled proudly.

"Why do you bring that up?" asked Jerry.

"Because I've run into more than one potential warlord on this journey," Frank said. "I just want to make sure that nobody feels they can take advantage. I have my eyes wide open. This isn't the wild west. This isn't the apocalypse. I will not give up my freedom to anybody – especially to somebody who says they are *only trying to protect me*."

"Well said, my friend," Jeb said. "I'm with you."

"Me too," Chester said.

"And me, sir," Jackson said. Earl was standing next to him nodding in agreement.

"And me," Arthur said.

"I think we all agree with you on that, Frank," Charlie said, "but it needed to be said. Thank you." Hilda got up next to Charlie and nodded as well.

"Here's the sign-up sheets," Hilda said, holding up two pieces of paper. "I made one for the blinds and one for the roof of the store. I'll leave them on this table. Come by at your leisure. Oh, and we'll have Happy Hour back here at 6:00pm. The drinks are on the house. We still have a lot of Charlie's spread left over....we'll put it out, so come hungry."

There was a smattering of applause.

People started slowly walking out of the clubhouse, and into the warm air outside. Jane grabbed Frank's hand and entwined fingers. He looked down at her.

"What?" he asked.

"I'm just proud of you, that's all," she said. "That's OK, isn't it?"

He smiled and nodded.

"That was a genius play," Jane said as they walked. "You were watching the crowd, weren't you? Most people were right there with you, but not all."

"I was watching the crowd, but I wanted to watch the folks up front."

"Really? I was a little worried about Jerry."

"Jerry is a loner, and he lacks social skills, which makes him seem abrupt and awkward. I'm not worried about him, though. I knew a lot of folks like him when I was running the IT department at work. Lots of computer scientists are like that."

"Go on," Jane said.

"You remember his joke when we were first exploring behind the park, right? It was a socially awkward comment. You also noticed his wife. You are right, she probably is something like a mail order bride."

"I think I know where you are going," Jane said. "He may ask questions, but he's not going to try to take over."

"Right. He's an introvert. He doesn't know how to meet women, and he's shy around most people. He's cautious and wary of people. He's not political. I want to get to know Jerry better, because he's probably really good at something. If it's IT, we could probably work together and put some security into this place that is a little less manpower intensive."

"What about the folks at the front of the room?"

"We need to watch Charlie and Hilda," Frank said. "I've already seen Charlie move in and try to steer things. He's very political. So is Hilda."

"You are worried about them? I don't see it," Jane said.

"I'm expecting them to try to put together some kind of leadership team or council," Frank said. "I'm going to fight that. When that happens, it will become a click, and people will start to become distrustful. Councils do things like banish people for breaking some arbitrary rule. If that happens here and we can't stop it, I think we'll want to move on."

"Well, it is Hilda's place, after all, and Charlie and she are, shall we say, *close*."

"Oh, you've picked up on that too, eh," Frank said with a smirk.

"More than that, I saw Charlie leaving her residence very early in the morning."

"Oh," Frank said. He chuckled. "Well, nothing wrong with that, but it is instructive."

"So who do you trust in this group?" Jane asked.

"Jeb. Chester. Arthur. Maybe Jerry. Maybe Earl and Jackson."

"Really, the two guys from the Williams militia?"

"Yes. And they may have been right about the police chief. That's been bothering me for a while. It was too tidy, and those three creeps came out of nowhere like that."

As they approached their rig, Lucy started barking. Jane and Frank looked at each other and laughed. Frank walked up to the door and unlocked it. He pulled it open and she bounded out, tail wagging, licking Frank's shins.

"Would you take her for a walk, honey?" asked Jane. "I want to freshen up a little bit."

"Sure," Frank said. He reached into the door and grabbed the leash and the poop bags. "Maybe we can go swimming when I get back."

"I have a chore for you to do first," she said, blushing. Frank picked up on it fast.

"Oh, really? Do tell," he said with a grin.

"Let's just say your speech had an effect on me," she said. Then she pulled the door closed, and Frank let Lucy drag him around the campsite.

{ 9 }

Happy Hour

Frank sat up in bed. He pulled the window blind aside and looked out. People were starting to meander over to the clubhouse for Happy Hour.

"Want to go, honey?" asked Jane. She was still lying in bed, a sheet covering her naked form.

"Yes, I think it would be good for us to go," Frank said. "Besides, you've worn me out. I need refreshment."

Jane picked up his pillow and threw it at him. Then she giggled.

"Oh, you want more, do you," Frank said, laughing. He jumped onto the bed next to her.

"Noooooo!" she said, still giggling. "Alright, I'm getting up."

Frank pulled her up and gave her a kiss. She melted into him.

"I love you, honey," Frank said.

She smiled up at him.

"Well, I guess I can tolerate you," she said. Then she giggled again.

"Oh, really?"

"Alright, I love you," she said. They kissed again, and then they got out of bed and got dressed.

"Wonder if they have any gin?" Frank asked.

"Martini night? Trying to take advantage of the best things in life, aren't you sir?"

"You only live once, and these are troubled times. You have to enjoy where you can."

"That almost sounded serious," Jane said, smirking.

"I was serious," Frank said. "And yes, I'm really enjoying us."

"Oh, shoot, I forgot to call Sarah," Jane said. She pulled out her phone and dialed as Frank was feeding Lucy and Mr. Wonderful.

"Sarah? It's mom."

"Hi, mom," Sarah said.

"Where are you, honey?"

"We only got to Boise before they called off the evacuation. We have been hanging out with my roommate's cousin. I think we're going to go back to Portland pretty soon."

"That's good, sweetie," Jane said. "I'm relieved. We were worried about you making the drive here, with the way things are."

"When are you and dad going home?"

"We don't know for sure. There are still a lot of problems in Arizona, and the southeastern border of California is still sealed up, from what we've heard. When we do go back, we'll probably come down from the north."

"Maybe you can see me on the way back."

"Yes, maybe we can, sweetie," Jane said. "Here, I'll hand the phone to your dad for a second."

"Alright, mom. I love you."

"Love you too, honey." Jane handed the phone to Frank.

"Here, say hello to Sarah. She didn't get past Boise....sounds like she's going back to Portland soon." Frank put the phone up to his ear.

"Hi, sweet pea," Frank said.

"Hi, daddy."

"So, you are in Boise?"

"Yeah, my roommate has a cousin that lives here who has put us up for a few days."

"Boy or girl."

Sarah sighed.

"He's a boy, daddy," she said. She giggled.

"I *see*," Frank said, trying to sound stern. "I think you'd better get back to Portland."

"Oh, daddy," she said. She giggled again.

"I'm just kidding, sweetie. I'm glad you didn't have to drive all the way to where we are. We were pretty worried about you making that trip."

"I know, but it was scary in Portland before we left. Looting and crazy stuff. It was good to be away for a little while. I'm not all that anxious to get back."

"Well, take your time then," Frank said. "Or even settle in Boise if you want to. What's holding you in Portland?"

"Nothing, really, come to think of it," Sarah said. "I have a job there, but it isn't a very good one. I could probably find as good a job here."

"Well, then think about it," Frank said. "We've got to go."

"OK, daddy, take care of mom," Sarah said. "I love you."

"Love you too, sweet pea," Frank said. "Bye bye."

Frank handed the phone back to Jane.

"She's interested in her roommate's cousin, I think," Frank said.

"I like that you suggested she stay in Boise," Jane said. "I think that's a better place for her."

"Me too," Frank said. "Ready to go?"

"Yes, let's go. And don't worry about drinking too many Martinis. I'll drive home."

Frank laughed. They went out the door, pushing Lucy back inside when she tried to follow them. Frank closed the door and locked it.

"I wonder what the cousin is like?" Jane asked.

"If he has a job and doesn't beat her, I'd be happy at this point," Frank said. "Some of her other boyfriends have been *interesting*, to say the least."

"Oh, stop it," Jane said, smirking. "She's a free spirit. I was one of those once."

"Last I checked you still were," Frank said. He put his arm around her shoulder as they approached the clubhouse.

Jane leaned her head against his shoulder as they walked through the door.

"Well, look at the love birds," Hilda said as they walked up. "I miss having a husband."

"Well, there's always Charlie," Jane said, wishing she wouldn't have when it came out of her mouth. Her face turned red.

"Oh, stop," Hilda said, putting her hand on Jane's shoulder. She got close so she could whisper. "Don't let on. I've almost got him hooked."

Jane got a big grin on her face.

"Mum's the word."

"Ah, Happy Hour," said a loud voice from over by the door. It was Rosie, beaming again. "Belly up, everybody!"

Jerry had a sheepish look on his face as he walked her in. Jasmine looked downright embarrassed.

Frank was already at the bar. Chester was bartending. They both turned and watched Rosie coming over.

"What will you have, Frank?" Chester said.

"Why don't you take care of Rosie first," he replied, grinning.

"Yes sir," Chester said.

"Wow, we have very handsome bartender, don't we," Rosie said.

"What will you have, beautiful?" Chester asked.

"Oh, and good liar too," Rosie said, grinning. "I'll take Weng Weng. You know how to make, young man?"

"Of course," Chester said.

"What's a Weng Weng?" asked Frank

"It's one powerful drink, from the Philippines," he said.

"Oh, yeah, baby," said Rosie. "Surprised you know what is. You can get in big cities, but out here, bartender don't know."

"What's in it?" Frank asked, chuckling.

"Almost everything back there," said Chester, waving his arm at the table behind him that was covered with booze bottles. "As I remember, it's ¾ ounce of Bourbon, Vodka, Tequila, Scotch, Brandy, and Rum, with a little OJ and Pineapple Juice, and a little Grenadine."

"Wow," Frank said. "Make that two. That will get me in the party mood in a hurry."

"You will like," Rosie said, smiling. "You Frank, right?"

"Yes, I'm Frank," he replied.

"You have lovely wife Jane?"

"Good memory," he said. "Yes, Jane is mine."

"How about bartender? Married?" she asked.

Chester looked up from the drinks and grinned.

"Confirmed bachelor, Rosie," Chester said. "Women don't tolerate me for very long."

They all laughed. Jerry walked up with Jasmine.

"Is she behaving?" asked Jerry.

"What you mean, behave," said Rosie. Then she cracked up.

"Rosie is a gem," Frank said. "Life of the party."

"Well, she is that, isn't she," Jerry said. He grinned.

Chester pushed the drinks across the bar, to Rosie and Frank. Rosie took a sip.

"You do very good," she said. "As good as Manila."

"Great, I aim to please," Chester said.

Frank took a sip, and shook his head.

"Wow," he said. "These things have some horsepower."

"Don't tell me, let me guess," Jerry said. "Weng Weng."

"Yep," Chester said. "Want one?"

He thought for a minute.

"Sure, why not. Guess we aren't driving anywhere."

"Coming right up, Jerry," Chester said. He got to work on another one.

"So Chester, where did you learn to tend bar?" asked Frank. "Didn't expect that."

"Here and there," he said. "Mostly in Nevada. Vegas, Reno, and Tahoe. Paid good, too, but they don't want you when you get too old. I had to hang it up when I couldn't move quick enough anymore."

"Were you in Vegas during the Rat Pack days?" asked Jerry, taking the first sip of his Weng Weng.

"Sure was," Chester said. "I knew most of those guys. Sinatra would talk your ear off. Joey Bishop was the funniest. Dino was the nicest. I really liked Dino. I got a Christmas card from him for years. So sad what happened to his boy."

"So what brought you to Williams?" Frank asked.

"I came home when I couldn't work anymore. My folks still had a little ranch there. I moved in with my brother."

"What happened to him?" Rosie asked.

"He passed on a few years back."

"Sorry to hear," she said.

"Oh, he lived a good long life," Chester said. "He was eight years older than me. Went in his sleep. I hope I go that way."

Jane and Hilda came walking up.

"Looks like you guys have the party going already," Hilda said, smiling.

"What will you have, girls?" Chester asked.

"Cosmo here," Hilda said. "How about you, Jane?"

"Martini, dry, with olives," she said.

"There's my girl," Chester said. He got to work on the drinks.

"What the devil is that you're drinking, Frank?" asked Jane, moving closer to him.

"This is a Weng Weng," Frank said, laughing. "Powerful stuff. Here, have a sip." He handed her the class and she took a careful sip. Then she shook her head.

"Wow.....that reminds me of the Hurricanes we had in New Orleans."

"Yep, pretty much," Frank said. "It's a drink from the Philippines."

"Ah ha, so Rosie is the bad influence here, huh," Jane said, laughing. Rosie looked at her and winked.

"So where's Charlie," asked Frank.

"He finally managed to get some people in his town on the phone," Hilda said. "He's talking to as many as he can get ahold of. He'll be along in a little while."

"Well, that's good," Frank said. "Should help us to gauge our safety here."

"Yes, that poor man is really worried about his RV Park," Hilda said. "It's been in the family for years. I don't want to see him leave, though."

"The place will probably keep pretty well," Frank said. "As I remember most of the buildings were made out of cinder block. Even if they get burned, it won't be a total loss."

"Yeah, he'd survive better than my place would," Hilda said. "Mine is mostly wood frame. My parents weren't very well off when they built this place."

"How old is this one?" asked Jerry.

"It was built in 1962. Not nearly as old as Charlie's place. His was built in the 1920s."

Chester slid the Cosmo and the Martini over to Hilda and Jane.

"Jasmine, would you like a drink?" Chester asked. "A Weng Weng, perhaps?"

Jasmine got a shy smile on her face.

"Those are too much for me. How about some white wine?" she asked.

"Coming right up," Chester said. He poured her a glass and gave it to her. She took a sip, then smiled and nodded.

"Thank you," Jasmine said. Then she looked over at Rosie. "How are you doing, mom?"

"I'm enjoying self," Rosie said. She was about halfway through her drink.

Jeb came strolling through the door. He was wearing dirty clothes. He walked up to the bar.

"Sorry, folks, I'll change later," he said. "Got any beer, Chester? I'm powerful thirsty."

"Care what kind?" Chester asked.

"Any American beer you have. Bud or Coors or Miller."

Chester pulled a Bud out of a tub of ice on the floor and handed it to him. Jeb popped off the top and drank about half of it in one gulp.

"Wow, you are thirsty," Hilda said, laughing. "What have you been up too?"

"You have someplace to store venison?" Jeb asked. "I just got one with my bow. It's been bled and cleaned, but I've still got some work to do."

"Of course, we can put some in the deep freeze and some in the walk-in fridge, assuming you are going to share."

"Of course," Jeb said. "I got it for the group. And by the way, very swanky blind back there. The booze and magazines are a nice touch."

Frank and Chester started laughing. Hilda just shook her head and smirked.

"Did you shoot the deer from the blind?" asked Jerry.

"No, too high up for bow hunting. It would be perfect for a rifle up there, but I would rather save the lead for protection if possible. Plus I didn't want to scare the devil out of all of you good people by firing my gun off."

"Well, that was very thoughtful, Jeb," Hilda said.

"So you had to stalk the deer on the ground," said Jerry. "Is that hard to learn?"

"Not really," Jeb said. "I'd be happy to teach anybody who is interested."

"That would be great," Jerry said. "I have a crossbow. I know they are kinda cheating."

"No they aren't, unless we are worried about when hunting season starts and finishes. Crossbows are a good way to learn."

"You know how to cook deer?" asked Rosie. She was starting to slur just a little bit.

"Why, yes, I do," Hilda said. "We used to have it all the time, and I used to serve it up to customers back when I had Jer to hunt it. It's as good as beef if you know how to cook it right. Maybe even better than beef."

"We won't starve here, that's for sure," Jeb said. "There's a lot of game out there. I saw some evidence of cougar when I was tromping around. You don't have those predators without some good game to support them."

"Yep, that's why Jer built those blinds," Hilda said.

"Well, I'd better get back to it," Jeb said. "I've got another hour of work to butcher the deer and clean up."

"Here, take one for the road," Chester said, handing Jeb another Bud. "I'll bring another one out to you in a little while."

"Thanks, that would be great," Jeb said. He walked out.

"Now there is a valuable guy to have around during times like these," Frank said.

"Yep, you can say that again," Jerry said.

"What do you do, Jerry?" asked Frank. "If you don't mind me asking."

"I'm a software engineer," he said. "I was working at that big missile plant down in Tucson before the crap hit the fan."

"Oh, that was part of Hughes Aircraft Company, right?" asked Frank.

"Yep, until it got sold. Miss that company."

"Me too," Frank said. "I worked at another division. We got sold to a different outfit."

"Really? What did you do?"

"I ran the IT department in El Segundo," Frank said.

"You aren't Frank Johnson, are you?" Jerry said.

"Sure am."

"I remember you," Jerry said. "I read one of your books. Good to meet you."

"Same here," Frank said. "Did you work system software?"

"Yes, guidance, mostly," he said.

"Here comes Charlie," Hilda said, looking over at the door. He walked over to the bar.

"How about a beer, Chester?" he said.

"Usual?" asked Chester.

"Sure," he said. Chester slid him a Coors. Charlie opened the can and took a large swig.

"What's Jeb up too?" saw him walking to the back of the park with a beer in his hand. He was a mess."

"He nailed a deer with his bow," Jerry said. "He's back there dressing it."

"Ah, should have guessed," Charlie said. "Love venison."

"So what's going on down south?" asked Frank.

"Oh, Hilda told you guys, huh?" Charlie asked.

"I told them the phones were back up," Hilda said.

"Good," Charlie said. "Alright, here's what I found out. Williams appears to be safe now. The Feds came in and kicked the militia types out, now that the Islamists are pretty much done. The Army chased the militia north. The bad news is that they are up in my neck of the woods now, hiding in the desert outside of Tusayan."

"Is you place alright?" asked Hilda.

"So far, yes, because it's too close to town for the militia folks. And get this. They are being chased by the last remaining Islamists."

"Really?" Frank asked. "Why?"

"Let's just say they did some things that were a rather big insult to the Prophet."

"Interesting," Jerry said. "I'll bet the Army is waiting for them to be in the same place, so they can clean up both messes."

"They aren't admitting to that, but the folks I talked to are thinking the same thing." Charlie said.

"Hmmmm," Frank said. "None of this is a total shock. Is the militia causing problems for people around Tusayan?"

"Yes, actually. They've been sneaking in at night to steal supplies, and they've kidnapped several girls. A fourteen year old, a sixteen year old, and a couple of women in their early twenties."

"Oh no," Jane said.

"Yeah, these are bad guys. The people I talked to are upset with the Army about this whole thing, because they won't come in and do anything until the Islamists get flushed out."

"I can't blame the locals for that," Hilda said. "What are they going to do?"

"Well, they would like to bring their daughters up here, but I advised against it. I suggested they take them down to Williams instead, since that is pretty well locked down."

"You didn't tell them where we are, I hope," Jerry said.

"No, and a couple of them are mad at me for that," Charlie said. "I'll have some fence mending to do when I can go back."

"Why you not tell them?" asked Rosie.

"The militia is still asking where we are. They want to avenge the 'Martyrs of Williams'."

"Do you think they'd drop what they are doing and come up here just to get to us?" asked Jane.

"Maybe," Charlie said. "I don't want to risk it."

"I think you did the right thing, Charlie," Chester said. "Another beer?"

"Sure, why not. Thanks, Chester."

"Anything on our old friend Officer Simmons?" asked Frank.

"I was getting to that. He's an interesting guy."

10

To Trust or Not To Trust

Frank was nervous, sitting at the bar, with people gathered around listening to Charlie. He had been on the phone with people in Tusayan, and was just getting to Officer Simmons.

"Has anybody actually talked with Officer Simmons there?" Frank asked.

"Yes. During the daylight hours, he has been around town asking questions. He's still wearing his uniform, but he's bandaged up around his torso, and limping. Most people are wary of him, but he's trying to convince them that he's there to help. They are also scared of the militia, because of what they've been doing, of course. Stealing supplies, moving into people's houses, and taking advantage of the women. Simmons has been asking for volunteers to take on the 'Williams Militia' as he calls them. He's not getting much response, though, even with the trouble the militia has caused. He tells tales about his raids against them, and his actions against the Islamists. His stories are pretty grisly, apparently. He tends to turn people off, and they don't believe him."

"This sounds similar to what Arthur was telling us," Chester said.

"For the most part, but I heard some things that make me think this guy isn't just after the Williams Militia."

"Really. What things?" asked Frank.

"He's telling the people in Tusayan that the Williams Militia broke into two pieces. Half of them are down around the Grand Canyon area outside of Tusayan, and the other half went north. He said that the person who shot him is with the people in the north, and he's going to get them after he neutralizes the people down there."

"Oh, crap," Frank said. Jane got closer to him. She was visibly shaken.

"The people in Tusayan know who came north," Chester said. "They know we aren't any damn militia."

"Yes, that's one of the reasons why the people down there are wary of this guy. The only people who will give him the time of day are the people who had their daughters kidnapped. Some of the others think this guy might have actually had something to do with the kidnappings. His stories never seem to add up."

"This guy bull crap," Rosie said. She was slurring her words now. "My Jerry kick his butt if he come here."

"Quiet, mom," Jasmine said softly. Jerry had a sheepish look on his face.

"Weng Weng," he said.

The woman who had the son in South Korea walked over. She was an older slender woman, with a spinster look about her, and long gray hair

"Hi, my name is Cynthia," she said. "I went to Arthur's rig to try to find out about my son."

"Oh, yes," Jane said. "Is he alright?"

"Yes, he was in the southern part of South Korea when the bombs went off. He is one of the humanitarian aid workers now."

"Good," Jane said. "So glad to hear that, Cynthia."

"Thank you," she said. "Arthur got the Regional Commander for Arizona on the radio when I was there. I heard the conversation. The commander said that the Islamists are all huddled together now, east of Flagstaff, and they will be rounded up over the next day or so. They may talk a big game, but they are tired and hungry now, and they surrender when they are caught. The leaders are all dead. There aren't a bunch of them chasing any militias around. The remaining Marxists from Venezuela are a bigger concern, and the Army is chasing them down into central Mexico now. They have North Korean heavy weapons, and they know how to use them. All the Islamists ever had was small arms."

"The Venezuelans aren't in the US anymore?" asked Jerry.

"Just stragglers, from what the commander was saying. They miscalculated in California. They didn't think the citizens would rise up and fight them. They didn't realize how crazy and stupid the Islamists were, either. They made the population mad with their convert or die nonsense. Once the people got mad, they pulled out their hunting rifles and just overwhelmed them."

"Sounds like whoever planned this mess was a real idiot," Jerry said.

"Yes," Cynthia said. "They made even bigger mistakes in Texas, and they sent a lot more Islamists over the Rio Grande down there. The commander was laughing about that. The Islamists were always trying to scare the people with insults. One of them was 'Crusader'…..and of course those Texans took that as a high complement. The Texas National Guard had to step between the people and the Islamists to stop the invasion from becoming a total bloodbath. The Islamists were fleeing to the west into New Mexico to escape the citizens, not the Army. Then, when they got out there, they had no idea how big and desolate it was going to be. Many of them died from the elements. Pretty funny when you think about it. They came from lands that were mostly desert, but they lived in villages or cities back there. Americans from the southwest are a lot better at living with this terrain and climate than they are."

"Yes!" Chester said. "Don't mess with Texas."

Charlie had a frustrated look on his face.

"You know that commanders are usually clueless about what is really happening on the ground," he said.

"No, I don't know that," Cynthia said.

"That's a lot of malarkey," Jerry said. "You ever been in the service, Charlie?"

"No," Charlie said, "but a lot of my friends have been."

"Well, I was in the Marines. Gulf War veteran. The entire chain of command flows detailed information from the ground up....and frankly, we have such good surveillance technology now that the commanders often have a better view of things than people on the ground. They can probably count the flies crawling around on the bad guy's helmets, especially in this country."

"Settle down, now, boys," Hilda said.

"Just having conversation," Jerry said. "I'm not angry, just telling what I've experienced. No hard feelings."

"So what do you think we ought to be doing?" asked Charley.

"Let's continue on the path that we are on," Jerry said. "It's a good one. Post people in the blinds to watch for scavengers. Have people watching the front of the park from the roof of the store. Be armed when leaving the park. Those are all sound measures. And above all, don't work ourselves into a panic."

"If you don't believe what the people in Tusayan are telling me, why even bother with posting people to watch?" asked Charlie.

"There are always bad folks looking to take advantage," Jerry said. "Remember the looting that was going on before the war got into full swing? People who do that aren't too bright, usually. When they think RV Park, they think helpless old people with stuff to steal. They rarely think it through any further. They rarely think self-reliant old people with guns."

Jeb was walking in, with clean clothes on now, and he heard the last comments by Jerry.

"You got that right," he said. "Chester, how about another beer?"

"Sure, here you go," Chester said as he slid one across the bar to him. Jeb opened it and took a big swig. "So what's going on in here? Kinda sounded like we had an argument starting up."

"No argument," Hilda said. "Just two different views of the situation."

"Oh?" asked Jeb.

"Yes," Frank said. "Charlie was able to get through to the people in Tusayan on the phone, and was telling us what they see happening down there. Cynthia was with Arthur last night, and he got the Regional Commander of Arizona on the radio."

"Oh, that's right, you were checking on your son in South Korea. How is he?" Jeb asked.

"He survived, thank God," Cynthia said. "Thanks for asking."

"Good, glad to hear it," he replied. "What's the difference in the stories? I'll bet what Charlie heard was a lot worse than what the commander said."

Everybody at the bar laughed except for Charlie and Hilda.

"I just put more stock in people on the ground than I do in people who are at the 50,000 foot level, that's all," Charlie said. "I know those folks in Tusayan. They aren't going to lie to me."

"So give me the nutshell edition for both," Jeb said. "I don't want to waste everybody's time with a full retelling of this."

"I can give you that," Frank said.

"Shoot."

"Charlie's sources said that the Williams Militia is active around Tusayan, and is being chased by a group of Islamists who were offended by some of their anti-Islamic actions and comments. Officer Simmons is down there too, raiding the Williams Militia as Arthur said yesterday, but he is also telling the locals that the Williams Militia broke into two pieces, and one of the pieces went north. He is telling them that the person who shot him is with the group that went north, and he's trying to get volunteers to fight both militia groups and the Islamists."

"Got it, so we would be in danger here if that was true," Jeb said. He looked over at Charlie and shook his head. "What about the commander?"

"He didn't actually contradict everything, just one very important thing. He said that the only Islamists left were hiding out east of Flagstaff, and they are surrendering as soon as the Army finds them. He also gave a lot of info on the wider conflict, but it didn't contradict anything that came out of Tusayan."

"You mean out of Charlie," Jeb said.

"Well, yes," Frank said.

"Now wait a minute, Jeb," Charlie said. "I wasn't lying."

"Didn't say you were, Charlie, just stating a fact," Jeb said dryly. "No offense meant. So what's the plan?"

"That's what Jerry was talking about when you walked in," Frank said. "He said that the current plan we have in place of posting people on watch in the blinds and on the roof of the store was a good plan, as is the policy of being armed when outside the park, due to scavengers."

"Ok, I get it," Jeb said. "And I agree with the reasons I was hearing when I walked in."

"Me too," Frank said. "Even if there is some truth to what the folks Tusayan are saying, I think we are on the right path. Do you agree, Charlie?"

"I think we ought to be more proactive, that's all," Charlie said. "I think we ought to get ourselves better organized, and perhaps even send a party down south to settle things."

"Now why would you want to do that, Charlie?" asked Jeb. "You aren't getting political aspirations again, are you?"

"I can't talk to this guy," Charlie said. "He hasn't changed since High School." He left the room.

"That wasn't very nice, Jeb," Hilda said.

"Look," Jeb said. "Charlie is my friend, and I would fight with him to the last man if we really needed to. He's also very ambitious. How many times did he run for office over the years?"

"He did win a couple of times, too, you know," Hilda said. "He was city councilman twice, and almost won for mayor back in 1998."

"I know, and he did a good job when he was in office," Jeb said. "This is different. I know where this is going. He figures he might be able to get himself famous, and then run for Congress or Senate or even Governor when this mess settles down."

"Is there anything wrong with that?" Hilda asked.

"Depends," Jeb said. "He's great at rallying people. He was captain of the football team, remember? I was on the team too. That's how we got so close back then. Nobody could motivate people like him. That is a valuable quality, but I don't want to see anybody risking their neck for him in this situation, unless they truly understand what they are doing and why."

"Oh, Jeb," Hilda said. "I think you are exaggerating a little bit."

"Maybe I was," Jeb said. "I'm tired and a little buzzed from the beer. We'll patch things up tomorrow. We always do."

Frank and Jane looked at each other. Jerry saw the look and came closer.

"Are you thinking what I'm thinking?" Jerry asked quietly.

"Probably," Frank said. "I saw this coming. That's why I made that little speech."

Jerry nodded.

Charlie came walking back in. He walked up to Jeb and shook hands with him.

"Sorry, old friend, I didn't mean to go off on you," he said.

"I'm sorry too, Charlie. I'm a little tired, and a little grumpy. Let's go have another beer."

"Heck yeah," Charlie said. They walked over to the bar. Chester had two beers out before they got there. Hilda saw them and came back over. She had a relieved smile on her face.

"Drink up," Rosie said, smiling. "Another drink, handsome?"

"You might not feel so good tomorrow if you have another of these things, Rosie," Jerry said, laughing. "This thing has got me on my butt."

"Good, you drink another too," Rosie said. "Two more Weng Weng please."

Chester cracked up.

"Coming right up, beautiful," he said. Then he winked at her. She patted her heart and pretended to swoon. Everybody at the bar started laughing again. Jasmine smiled, and put her arm around Jerry.

"Ah, let her have fun," Jasmine said. Jerry nodded. Then he looked over at Frank.

"Want to go have a cigar? I've got some good ones," he asked.

"Sure," Frank said. He looked at Jane and she nodded. The two of them went outside to the porch.

"Here you go," Jerry said, handing a long cigar to Frank. Frank put it into his mouth and Jerry pulled out his lighter and got it going.

"Haven't had one of these in a few years," Frank said. "I missed them."

Jerry got his lit, and nodded.

"Yes, this is my guilty pleasure," he said. "So, what do we do now?"

"Well, I think we do exactly what we planned to do with the posting of watches, and we keep an eye on things. We resist efforts at further organizational hierarchy in our group."

"And we get our info from short wave," Jerry said.

"Yes. We should have Arthur show a few of us how to run his radio, too."

"I already know how. I'm a ham operator myself, but I didn't bring my equipment. I was a communications expert in the service...I could probably even fix the thing if it breaks down."

"Good to know," Frank said. He took a puff of the cigar and coughed a little bit. Both of the men snickered.

"Wonder where Arthur was tonight? I didn't think he would miss this little get together. He seems pretty gregarious."

"He's a little frail. He probably just stayed home to relax."

"Probably," Jerry said. He took another puff. "Glad I brought plenty of these."

"They are pretty good," Frank said.

"So how much of Charlie's story do you buy?"

"I believe that there are still some remnants of the Williams Militia out there, and I believe that Officer Simmons is still out there. We had already heard about that from Arthur. I don't believe much else. The Islamist story is probably a fabrication."

"It's possible that there are rumors like that floating around Tusayan," Jerry said. "You know how people get."

"I know that's a possibility, and I'd like to give Charlie the benefit of the doubt as long as I can. We'll be able to tell what's what by his actions, I think. I doubt that it will take long."

"Do you buy what Jeb was saying? Or is this really about getting folks together to go secure Charlie's RV Park?"

"I believe what Jeb was saying," Frank said. "I've been watching Charlie. He always has to be at the center of everything. I could understand that when we were at his park, but now? Notice how Hilda defers to him?"

"They have a thing going on," Jerry said. "Jasmine has seen some things."

Frank chuckled.

"So has Jane," he said. "Late night visits and such."

"Not that there's anything wrong with that, of course," Jerry said. "More power to them."

"Agree," Frank said. "They have history. She dated both Charlie and Chester in her youth."

"Yeah, I heard something about that."

Somebody came out of the door. It was Cynthia. She walked over to them.

"Oh, I love that smell," she said. "Reminds me of my late husband."

"Really?" Jerry asked. "How long has he been gone?"

"Going on six years now, rest his soul," she said.

"Sorry he's gone," Frank said.

"Me too, but that's the way of things, you know. He was quite a bit older than me."

"Jasmine will probably be in the same situation eventually," Jerry said. "Especially if I continue to smoke these things."

"She's a beautiful girl, Jerry," Cynthia said.

"Yes, and I love her mother too," Jerry said with a grin.

"Rosie knows how to have a good time, that's for sure," Cynthia said.

"Yes, she does," Frank said. "Nice lady."

"Yes," Cynthia said. "Have either of you heard anything from Arthur? He told me he was going to be here."

"No, but we were wondering where he was too," Frank said. "He looks pretty frail. Maybe he just got tired. Things have been a little crazy over the last several days."

"Maybe, but I think I'm going to go check on him," Cynthia said. "Talk to you two later." She walked down the steps of the porch and off into the park. It was almost completely dark now.

"She's a nice lady," Jerry said. "She was pretty quiet at first, but she seems to be coming out of her shell now. She's very sharp for her age, too."

"How old do you think she is?"

"I'm guessing early 80s at least."

Suddenly there was a scream. Frank and Jerry both looked in that direction, and went running out into the darkness. They saw Cynthia staggering down the steps of Arthur's coach, crying.

"What happened?" asked Frank.

"Arthur is dead," she said, sobbing.

11

Was it Murder?

Cynthia collapsed against the side of Arthur's motor home, tears streaming down her face. Frank and Jerry ran over to her and steadied her. They walked her over to a chair that was under Arthur's awning, and sat her down. She was sobbing.

"I can't believe he's dead," she said.

"We better get in there," Frank said to Jerry. He nodded, and they went up the steps into Arthur's rig.

"Jerry, don't tell anybody else that you know how to operate the radio," Frank said quietly.

"I was thinking the same thing," he replied.

Arthur was laying on the couch. It looked like he was watching TV when something happened….it was still on.

"Look, Frank," Jerry said, looking closely at Arthur's face. "See the indentations? There was a pillow pushed against his face." He pulled out his cellphone, got really close, and took several pictures with the flash on. "I don't know if this will show up. Wish I still had my old SLR."

"Are you saying that somebody smothered him?" asked Frank.

"That would be my guess. Where's the pillow?" He looked around, and saw one sitting on the floor between the front seats of the rig. He pointed. Frank went over to it.

"Stop," Jerry said. "Let me take pictures before you move anything." Frank nodded as Jerry came over and took a few shots.

"Good enough?" Frank asked. Jerry nodded. Frank picked up the pillow. "Is this the pattern you are seeing?"

"Yes, that looks like it. Either somebody smothered him, or he was laying on this, and went into convulsions that caused the pillow to fly over here."

"We'd better ask Cynthia if she moved anything."

"Good point," Jerry said. They turned to walk down the steps. Cynthia was still in the chair. She had stopped crying, and looked up at them as they approached.

"Cynthia, are you alright?" asked Frank.

"Yes, but that was a shock," she said.

"Did you move anything in the rig? A pillow, perhaps?"

"No, I didn't touch anything. Why? Do you think there was foul play?"

"No, I doubt it. It's probably nothing," Jerry said.

"Good Lord, I hope he wasn't murdered," Cynthia said. "It will be hard to feel safe if that happened."

"Yes," Frank said. "Let's not say anything like that. We don't want to get everybody upset."

"What should we do? Call the sheriff?" asked Cynthia.

"I think we had better," Jerry said. "I hope we aren't on our own."

"I'm going to call 911 right now, and then we should go let Hilda know," Jerry said. He dialed on his phone and the operator picked up after a couple of rings. Jerry gave a thumbs up.

"Good," Cynthia said. Frank nodded.

"Hello," Jerry said. "I need to report a death at the RV Park off of Highway 89, near Capitol Reef and Bryce Canyon."

"Hope they can send somebody out tonight," Frank said.

"Yes, me too," Cynthia replied.

"Hello, Sheriff Brown. We have a death in an RV at the park......yes, Hilda's park. And older gentleman..........his first name is Arthur........no, I don't know his last name."

Jerry hung up the phone.

"They are on their way," Jerry said. "Should be here in about twenty minutes."

"Alright, then I'll go tell Hilda. Maybe you two should hang out here until the Sheriff arrives."

"Agreed," Jerry said. Cynthia nodded.

"Be back in a few minutes," Frank said. He turned and left.

The party was still going on at the clubhouse. Everybody in there was gathered around Rosie, who was telling a story. Hilda saw Frank come in the door. He motioned for her to come over. She headed towards him.

"Something wrong?" asked Hilda.

"Cynthia went out to check on Arthur, because he told her he was coming to Happy Hour. She found him dead in his rig."

Hilda put her hand over her mouth, and her eyes got wide.

"Oh, no, that poor man," she said.

"Jerry already called 911, and Sheriff Brown is on his way out."

"Thank you," Hilda said. "It doesn't look like foul play, does it?"

"I wouldn't want to say," Frank said. "I'll let the sheriff look at it."

"He was rather frail," Hilda said. "We've had folks pass here before. It's so sad when that happens. How did you find out?"

"Jerry and I were out on the porch smoking cigars when Cynthia asked us if we had seen him. She was worried so she went to check on him. We heard her scream when she found him, so we ran over."

"Oh," Hilda said.

"Well, I'm going to go out there and wait for the Sheriff with Cynthia and Jerry. I'm sure they will want to question us."

"Alright. Should I say anything to the crowd?"

"Why don't you wait until after the Sheriff has been here," Frank said.

"OK, but I will let Charlie know. I'll take him in the office and tell him."

Frank nodded, and she left. Jane was looking at Frank, so he motioned her over.

"What's cookin?" asked Jane.

"Arthur is dead in his rig," Frank said quietly. Jane's eyes grew wider.

"No," she said. "Natural causes?"

"Not sure yet. The sheriff is on his way over here. I'm going back out to the rig."

"Who found him?"

"Cynthia. She's pretty shook up."

"I could imagine. Are you going to tell the others?"

"No, but I just told Hilda. I told her it might be a good idea to hold off on making a big announcement until the Sheriff has been here."

"She told Charlie, I'm guessing. I saw them go into the office together before I got to you."

"Yes, she said she was going to do that."

"You think there was foul play, don't you?" she asked.

"It looks a little suspicious to Jerry. I'm not sure. I hope the old guy just vapor locked."

"Me too," Jane said. "I'll go with you out there."

Frank nodded, and they headed back to Arthur's rig. When they got there, Cynthia and Jerry were sitting on the chairs, silently.

"How did Hilda take it?" asked Cynthia.

"Shock. She'll be out her in a few minutes, probably with Charlie," Frank said.

"Do you guys trust Charlie?" asked Cynthia.

Frank and Jerry looked at each other.

"I don't think we should go there right now," Jane said, watching the situation. "He's going to be out here with Hilda in a few minutes, and the Sheriff will show up soon too."

"It's just that he got mad when I contradicted him with the stuff Arthur and I heard."

"I know," Jerry said. "Frank and I are wondering about that too. But let's not jump to any conclusions. Let's let the sheriff look at things."

Hilda was on her way out to the rig, with Charlie.

"We'd better hush up, here they come," Cynthia said.

"You guys called the sheriff already, huh," Charlie said. "Maybe we should have talked about it first." Hilda stood silently next to him, looking down, somber.

"Why?" asked Frank. "It's not like anybody needs to get their story straight here."

"Don't misunderstand me," Charlie said. "I don't think anybody here killed him. I just think we ought to talk before we bring in outsiders."

"There are no 'outsiders'......we aren't a country. We aren't a militia either," Frank said. "We aren't even a club. We are a bunch of people who found ourselves on the road together, and we are all customers of Hilda's park. We can cooperate when it is in our interest, but we aren't a group that has to prepare for a visit by the sheriff. We don't have to ask permission to call 911 if we find that somebody has passed away, either."

"Let's not get ourselves into a tizzy," Hilda said. She looked over at Frank. "Charlie didn't mean any harm. He's just concerned that things may get out of our control."

Frank started to respond, but Jane put her hand on his forearm, and looked him in the eye. She shook her head no.

"I wonder if anybody else knows how to run the radio?" asked Charlie.

Jerry and Frank looked at him silently.

"It's important, guys," Charlie said. "That was our link to the outside world."

"The phones are back up, remember?" Jerry said.

"We never did lose the TV stations or the commercial radio, either," Frank said. "Worse comes to worse, we can go into town and talk to people."

"Yeah, I know, this isn't the apocalypse," Charlie said sarcastically. "We are only at war on the US mainland for the first time since the Civil War."

"Now all of you stop it," Hilda said. She was on the verge of tears.

"Ever read 'Lord of the Flies'? Or 'Animal Farm'?" Frank asked.

There were headlights coming through the front gate. All of them turned and looked in that direction. Hilda stood up and waved to the sheriff's car. It slowly made its way out to them, and parked on the road in front of Arthur's space. A large man got out of the driver's seat, and closed the door. A much smaller young man got out of the passenger seat. They walked over.

"Hi, Hilda, how are you," asked the sheriff. "Sorry to see you under such sad circumstances."

The younger man came walking over.

"Hi, Hilda," he said.

"Who are these folks?" asked the sheriff.

"Guests," Hilda said. "That's Frank and his wife Jane, Jerry, and Cynthia. You probably already know Charlie."

"Of course," he said. "I'm Sheriff Jack Brown, glad to meet you folks. This is Deputy Terry Clark."

"The gentleman who passed is in that rig. Cynthia found him," Hilda said.

"Anybody else go in?" asked Sheriff Brown.

"Jerry and I went in after Cynthia told us," Frank said. "We didn't move anything around."

"Good. C'mon, Terry, let's go take a look." They both climbed the steps into the coach. The coach moved slightly as Sheriff Brown moved around. Lights in the back of the coach came on, and then more lights up in the front. They came back out after a few minutes.

"Looks like natural causes to me," Sheriff Brown said. "Nice short wave setup. He was probably your eyes and ears, wasn't he?"

"Well, to a certain extent," Frank said. "Are you sending out the coroner?"

"Yes, I'm going to radio them now. The Deputy is looking at the ham radio. He knows short wave. The power switch is on, but the radio isn't working. We are wondering a bit about that."

"Maybe a fuse blew in the coach," Charlie said.

"Maybe. They do pull some current," Sheriff Brown replied. "I'm not a ham operator myself, but they did teach us about them in one of our continuing education classes."

"Ah, they make you guys take those too, huh," Jerry said. "I learned how to fix radios in the service. If the Deputy can't get it going again, I'd be happy to take a look at it."

"What branch were you in?" asked the Sheriff.

"Marines," Jerry said, a look of pride coming over his face.

"Semper fi," said the Sheriff. "Me too. Always glad to meet a brother." He walked over and shook hands with Jerry.

"Likewise, sir," Jerry said.

"See action?"

"Gulf War," Jerry said.

"Really? Me too," the sheriff said. "Would have gotten back in for Afghanistan, but they wouldn't let me. Too old and too fat."

Both men started cracking up.

The Deputy came out of the coach, shaking his head.

"Well, it's not something simple. Not a fuse in either the radio or the coach, from what I can tell."

"Jerry here says he knows how to work on them," the Sheriff said. "Get on the horn and call for the coroner, alright?"

"On it, Jack," he said, as he walked towards the vehicle. He opened the passenger side door, got in, and got on the radio.

"So what happens now?" asked Charlie.

"We'll write up a report, and take some pictures," the Sheriff said. "The coroner will take the body away. Did any of you know the gentleman well?"

"No, not really," Hilda said. "He was just a fellow traveler."

"Alright, then we'll get his name and address via the registration for his coach, and see if he has any next of kin."

"Is it alright if I take that radio and see if I can fix it?"

"Sure, just remember where you got it," the Sheriff said. "I'm sure his family will want all of his stuff. Hilda, I'm going to give you the keys…..please keep this locked up until you hear from me."

"Of course, Jack," Hilda said.

"They are on their way," the Deputy said, coming towards them. "We lucked out, they were close by. Ought to be here in about five minutes."

"Sheriff, will you come in the coach while I take the radio? I want to make sure you see what I take," Jerry said.

"Of course," he said, and they both climbed up the steps into the coach. Frank looked over and could see them talking through the window. Then he saw Jerry point to the pillow up in the front section. Then he walked over to where the radio was, unplugged some wires, and picked it up. He carried it out of the coach, and the Sheriff followed him. He had a grim look on his face.

Jerry set the radio down on the picnic table next to the coach, and came back over to where the group was standing.

"Well, I'm going to go back to the clubhouse, before people start getting worried and start showing up out here," Charlie said. "Is it OK to tell them what happened?"

"I don't see why not," the Sheriff said. "Just make sure that you tell them it was natural causes. We don't want people getting nervous."

"Agreed," Charlie said.

"Should I go too, Charlie?" asked Hilda.

"If they don't need you here," he said.

"You can go, Hilda," the Sheriff said. "We'll take it from here."

The couple walked back to the clubhouse. About the time they got there, lights shined through the gate, and the coroner's wagon drove through. The Deputy walked over to the Sheriff's car and switched on their top lights. The wagon made its way over.

"Alright, folks, no need for you to stick around," the Sheriff said. "We'll lock up and drop the keys off with Hilda on the way out."

"Thanks, Sheriff Brown," said Jerry. "I'll take this radio back to my rig, and then hit the clubhouse to pick up my girls." Cynthia and Jane and Frank all nodded, and they walked back towards the clubhouse as Jerry picked up the radio. They got there just as Hilda and Charlie were about to make the announcement.

"Can we have your attention, please?" asked Hilda in a loud voice. A hush came over the room, and Hilda looked over at Charlie. He stood up.

"I'm afraid we have some sad news, folks. Arthur has passed away in his coach. The Sheriff and the Coroner are out there now."

There was a murmur going through the crowd.

"How did he die?" asked Jasmine. Rosie came over close to her, trying to steady herself against her daughter.

"Natural causes, from the look of it," Charlie said. "He was an old gentleman. This is something that happens at RV parks on occasion, as most of you know."

"Yep, get a bunch of oldsters together often enough and it's bound to happen," Jeb said. "A toast to Arthur. Happy Trails. You will be missed."

About half the people in the room raised their glasses.

"I think maybe we should call it a night," Hilda said.

"Agreed," Charlie said.

"Are we posting guards tonight?" asked Jeb.

"Maybe we should wait a day or two," Charlie said.

"Well, I'll tell you what. I could use a few more drinks. Maybe I'll just mosey up into that nice blind and kick back for a while."

"Your choice, Jeb," Hilda said. "Just don't get too drunk and fall out of there. We don't need the coroner coming back here."

"Don't worry, Hilda," he said. Then he walked out of the room.

The crowd slowly flowed out the door, murmuring softly. Jerry came in through the door, against the stream of people flowing out, and made his way to Jasmine and Rosie. Jasmine rushed to him and hugged him tightly. Rosie walked over and put her hand on Jerry's shoulder. They turned and walked out together. Jane and Frank were the last couple to leave.

"Alright, Frank, what are you thinking?" Jane asked as they walked along.

"When Jerry and I were in the coach, he pointed out some marks on Arthur's face that matched the pattern of the pillow," he said.

"Oh oh."

"I looked, but couldn't really see what he was talking about. Probably my eyes.....he's a lot younger than I am. And it was dim in the coach."

"You don't sound like you completely buy the idea that this wasn't just natural causes."

"I'm just trying to be cautious," Frank said. "I know that Jerry told the Sheriff what he thinks."

"How do you know that?"

"I could see him through the window of the coach, when he was in there with the Sheriff getting the radio. He pointed to Arthur's face, and then pointed to the throw pillow."

"Really. Well, that's good, isn't it?"

"Yes, I think so," Frank said. "If there's something to it, the Sheriff will figure that out."

Lucy started barking when she heard them approach.

"There goes our burglar alarm," Jane said, laughing. Frank unlocked the door and opened it, and Lucy jumped out.

"I'll get her leash and take her out," Frank said. He reached into the coach and grabbed it. Then he hooked it to Lucy's collar.

"Alright, I'll go in and get us ready for bed," Jane said.

Frank and Lucy walked around. It was quiet now. People had gotten back to their rigs, and he saw lights turning off in some of them. He could see Jerry's coach across the road and down about 50 yards. His lights were still on.

Lucy finished her business and Frank brought her back into the coach. Jane was sitting on the couch in her nightgown, watching a little bit of Fox News.

"Anything interesting?" Frank said as he closed and locked the door.

"Egypt and Israel have really clobbered the Islamists," Jane said. "That's all that I've seen so far."

"Well, that's good news," Frank said, sitting down next to her. "That Happy Hour was lots of fun before the stuff with Arthur came up."

"Yes, it was," Jane said. "It's lucky for you that you went outside with Jerry, or you probably would have had another one of those Weng Weng things. I'll bet Rosie won't feel very good tomorrow. Enjoy the cigar?"

"It was alright. I didn't like it enough to go back to those things. My mouth and throat feel dirty."

"I can smell it," Jane said. "So what did you guys really go out there for?"

"He wanted to discuss the stuff that Charlie told us, and the stuff that Cynthia and Jeb said."

"I take it he trusts Charlie about as much as you do."

"Yes. We were discussing the short wave radio when Cynthia came over."

"What did she want?"

"She asked if we had seen Arthur. He told her that he was coming to the Happy Hour, and he never showed up. She was worried. She left us to go check on him. You know the rest."

"Poor lady," Jane said. "What a terrible thing to find. Does she know what Jerry thinks about this?"

"Not sure. Jerry made some comments, but was careful not to say much in front of her. She's smart, though. She might have picked it up."

Lucy stood up and started to growl. Then she started barking. Frank got up and looked out the window.

"It's Jerry, better put on your robe."

Jane got up and went into the bedroom. Frank opened the door and Jerry climbed in.

"What's up, Jerry?"

"Somebody disabled that radio on purpose. They knew exactly what they were doing."

To be continued in Bugout! Part 3!

ABOUT THE AUTHOR

Robert G Boren is a writer from the South Bay section of Southern California. He writes Short Stories, Novels, and Serialized Fiction.

Made in the USA
Lexington, KY
27 July 2018